KICK
THE CAN

Also by Jim Lehrer

KICK
THE CAN

Jim Lehrer

G. P. Putnam's Sons
New York

G. P. Putnam's Sons
Publishers Since 1838
200 Madison Avenue
New York, NY 10016

Library of Congress Cataloging-in-Publication Data

Lehrer, Jim.
Kick the can.
I. Title.
PS3562.E4419K5   1988   813'.54   87-19192
ISBN 0-399-13350-X

Printed in the United States of America
1   2   3   4   5   6   7   8   9   10

To Kate

KICK
THE CAN

1
To Be a Pirate

I was too old to play kick-the-can anymore so I was just standing there watching when Jimmy T. came running in from behind our house. He kicked the can as hard as he could. It flew up toward me and the ragged part of the lid caught my left eye. It tore it halfway out of the socket. There was a lot of bleeding and crying and when it was all over at St. Joseph's Hospital I had lost my left eye forever.

The worst part was that I was going to our junior college in the fall so I could be a Kansas State Highway Patrolman like my dad. He was the best state trooper in Kansas and from the time I could talk and think I wanted to be one like him. He had talked to me over and over about what it meant to be a man of the law on the roads and highways of Kansas. I played with his badge and wore one of his old dark-blue uniform hats in the shape of a Royal Canadian Mounted Policeman's and put handcuffs on my sister and my friends a lot.

My favorite main dream was the Trooper Dream. I could

close my eyes anywhere anytime and bring it up across my mind like a biology slide at school. Usually I was chasing somebody in my trooper car at full Code 3 with the siren blasting and red light flashing. Sometimes there would be an armed gang to apprehend single-handedly. Or an escaped convict with a hostage, a bank robber who really wanted to go straight, a beautiful girl who had lost her way to find the sick father she had not seen since she was a little girl. Occasionally I was wounded but never more than a flesh wound and it always ended happily and heroically for me, the Trooper.

My sister Meg was there at the hospital with Dad right after they brought me in. She cried. She always cried when things went wrong. Dad told me almost right away I couldn't be a state trooper anymore. "It takes two eyes to do that, son," is the way he put it when I asked him. He was tall and handsome and had a deep voice like he was talking into a water glass. "It takes two eyes to do that, son."

I didn't even know how to dream about being anything else.

Until my glass eye came I wore a black leather patch over the empty left eye socket. Everybody said it made me look like a pirate, but I figured I just looked like a sixteen-and-a-half-year-old guy without a left eye.

The first thing I thought about doing after I got out of St. Joseph's Hospital was to find Jimmy T. and kill him. I'd get the same tin can and take that lid and maybe slit his throat or cut an ear off, if nothing else. The problem with that was, he came to see me at the hospital and he cried and said he was sorry and wished he could give me his left eye to replace mine.

The second thing I thought about was killing myself. Not with the tin can but maybe by lying down in front of the

1:22 Sante Fe doodle bug, our only passenger train. I thought about it so much it caused bad dreams. Once I was lying on the tracks naked and the doodle bug came down the track but, lo and behold, head cheerleader and Miss Posture Perfect Lisa Andrews was the engineer. Instead of running over me she just laughed at me and my various bodily parts. I got up and ran before the train got there but I couldn't get away. It kept coming and she kept laughing until I woke up.

The worst dream was when the train ran over me like it was supposed to but it cut off only my head. My body from the neck down ran off but my head stayed there next to the track, saying, "All aboard for Wichita! All aboard for Wichita!" Both of the dreams pretty well did away with my desire to kill myself.

So I went on to junior college and decided to make The Thunderbird my life's work. The Thunderbird was Thunderbird Motor Coaches, the wonderful bus company that went through town. I needed two eyes to be a bus driver but I figured one was fine for working as a ticket agent at the bus depot. One of my dad's best friends was a Thunderbird driver and Dad took me to coffee with him a lot at the depot café. I liked the people there and the smell and the sound of the buses. I would also get a pass so I could go free anywhere Thunderbird went anytime I wanted to.

The only problem, it turned out, was Thunderbird. They wouldn't hire me. Junior Dillard was the depot manager. He never looked at me and said, "You've only got one eye, so please go away." I'm sure that was it, though. I had spent the two years in junior college hanging around the bus depot at night and on weekends and Junior Dillard knew it. He knew the night agent, a nice man named Molina, had taught me how to read schedules and make out baggage checks and tickets. Making out a ticket is not as easy as it sounds. You have to do a coupon for each change of bus, and going from here to Baltimore, Maryland, say, means six separate coupons. The first one to Wichita and then another to Kansas City and one each from there to St. Louis, to Indianapolis, Indiana, to Washington, D.C., and finally, to Baltimore. Knowing the best route is one of the many jobs of the ticket agent.

Junior Dillard. What kind of name was Junior Dillard for a Thunderbird bus depot manager to have, anyhow?

I felt like I used to feel when I was playing ball. Our high school was Carrie Nation Memorial High School in honor of the no-drinking lady who went around Kansas busting up saloons with a hatchet. Our nickname was The Hatchets. The Carrie Nation Hatchets. The coach said go up there to the plate and hit it out of here like Stan the Man Musial. I'd go up there and swing as hard as I could but it hardly ever went out of here. I was fine in the field—second base, mostly— but when the pitcher curved me I swung and I usually missed.

I felt like somebody was curving my life.

That's when I decided to be a pirate. I knew very little about pirates. Only that there were good ones and bad ones. The bad kind stuck knives in their mouths and boarded helpless ships and hurt helpless people. The good kind were those in an operalike thing called *The Pirates of Penzance* the junior college chorus put on once. The pirates sang and laughed and acted more like Robin Hoods than real pirates. Those were my kind. I would not hurt anyone.

It was a crazy thing to think about in the year 1949. But I could not think of anything else right then.

The most important thing was that one eye was all I would need and I could even put the black patch back on. I hated the glass eye. They didn't get the shade of brown right so it was lighter than the brown in my real right one. Also, it didn't move like the real right one. It was like having a dead marble up there for everybody to stare at.

There was no way to be a pirate in Kansas. There were a couple or so lakes around and the Arkansas River was there but they just wouldn't work. I went to the library and looked at the Rand McNally Road Atlas and decided the best place that was closest would be down at the end of Texas. They had an ocean down there called the Gulf of Mexico that would be fine. The librarian said there had definitely been pirates in a place called Galveston.

"What did the pirates do there?" I asked.

"Mostly killed people and stole things that didn't belong to them," she said.

"Didn't they kill only evil people and give what they stole to the poor?"

"Only in the movies," she said.

What did she know?

First I had to get some money for the trip to Texas and a little extra to live on while I got started as a pirate. I checked the train because I wasn't about to give any of my money to Junior Dillard. I could catch the 1:22 Sante Fe doodle bug to Newton, change to the Texas Chief streamliner and go right on down to Galveston. The fare was $15.75.

So I took a job with the county road department for forty-six dollars a week. A deputy sheriff who was a friend of Dad's made sure I got it. I didn't have to pay to sleep or eat at home so I figured I should have enough saved up in seven months to head out. Seven months from then would take it to April.

April Fool, Galveston, Texas! Here I come in seven months!

I hated the road job at first. They put me in a blacktop crew. Every morning at 6:45 four of us and a truck with a tank of hot asphalt went out and sprayed county roads. That stuff got into my hair and nose and ears and every evening I came home looking like I'd been swimming in a Arkansas River of tar. I even had to take out the glass eye every night and scrub it down in the bathroom sink with Lux.

After six weeks of that I was switched to a mowing crew and that was much better, because driving a tractor with a mower on it or even out there tossing a hand sickle at the thick and tall weeds wasn't as awful and messy as that black stuff.

My mother would have been happy for me and my clothes if she had been around then. She died when I was twelve years old. She woke up one morning with a terrible pain in her stomach and the doctor came and looked at her. He said it was probably just bad indigestion or an ulcer at worst. But it did not get better, and four days later her fever shot up and Dad picked her up in his arms and took her to the hospital in his state police car, Code 3, with the red light flashing and the siren wailing. They said her fever was almost to 107 by the next morning and she died just before lunch. She had a burst appendix and Dad said that if the doctor had called it right the first day and taken her to the hospital she would not have died. I don't think he ever said anything to the doctor about it, though. I would have. Meg, my sister, who is two years older than me, cried for eight straight days after Momma died. It was a scary, awful cry that sounded more like a dog or a coyote than an older sister.

I cried the first night and the afternoon after the funeral

at the Methodist church and again six weeks later when I woke up in the morning with a sore throat and realized Momma wouldn't be there to look down it, give me some hot saltwater to gargle, and call the school and tell them I wasn't coming today.

My momma loved me very much and I would do anything to keep that love. She and Dad met when she was working as a clerk in Justice of the Peace Wilbert's office in Emporia and Dad was a new young trooper. Dad said he knew from the first moment he saw her that she was going to be able to twist him in knots and untie him and twist him again and again and again forevermore. Forevermore just didn't turn out to be very long. For me either.

It's hard not to wonder if I would have turned out differently if she had not died when I was twelve. And what if Junior Dillard had hired me at The Thunderbird? What if I hadn't gone out to watch them play kick-the-can?

Questions like that can drive you crazy.

I could not tell my dad and sister that I was going off to Texas to be a pirate. They wouldn't have understood even if I had explained it to them, which I couldn't have anyhow. So I just snuck away.

It was April 6, a Thursday, and I had saved $273. That would get me to Galveston fine and keep me there until I got established. I chose Thursday to leave because Dad always patrolled U.S. Highway 81 up toward McPherson then, and my sister took her afternoon break at the bank just after one o'clock on Thursdays. She was the relief teller at the Farmers and Drovers State Bank and her hours were different every day.

I walked in her bank just after one o'clock and got my $273 out of savings. I went from the bank straight to the train station seven blocks away just in time to jump on the doodle bug.

The only things I had taken with me were a few sets of underwear, three shirts, a pair of extra pants, some socks, a toothbrush and razor, plus some pictures and a couple of special items. I stuffed it all into a white shopping bag Mom had used to put her sewing in. On the sides it had the name of the biggest department store in Kansas, Roebaugh-Buck's. I had on a pair of dark blue corduroy pants, a light blue Montgomery Ward dress shirt and a brown sweater that used to be Dad's.

The Sante Fe doodle bug looked like a doodle bug and ran like a bus on tracks. It was just two railroad cars with a motor up front in the first one. There were three passengers in that first car with the engineer and conductor when I got on, so I went on to the second where there was nobody. I didn't want anybody to see me do what I was going to do.

I waited until I had given the conductor my ticket. He was back up front and we were just a few miles out of town when I raised a window. I reached up and took my glass eye out of the left socket, held it and looked at it a second. Then I threw it out of that window as hard as I could. Good-bye to you, forever!

The last I saw of it, it was landing in some tall brown grass like it was comfortable and it belonged there.

I put the window back down and took my black eyepatch out of my Roebaugh-Buck's bag. I put the string strap up over my head and the patch over that left socket. I took out Dad's old trooper hat, the one that looked like a Mountie's.

I had pinned the brim up and back like a pirate captain would wear it.

I put it on and smiled and felt good.

It was the first time I had smiled and felt good in the over three years since Jimmy T. kicked that can up in my eye.

2
Pepper

I wanted seeing Texas for the first time to be something really special. I wanted five friendly, fearless outlaws with long-barreled pistols and long white cowboy coats to ride their palomino horses alongside the Texas Chief streamliner train at top speed until they got the engineer to stop. I wanted them to come into the coach where I was and one of them to say, nicely, "Welcome to Texas, ladies and gents. Can we please have your paper and silver money, your gold and your watches, your diamond and graduation rings, your jade and ID bracelets and your pearl and native necklaces, so we may help feed the poor and needy of our state? Thank you." I wanted them then to file among us as we happily put our valuables in their hats. I wanted the tallest and smartest of them, who walked like a starting pitcher, to turn back at the car door to me.

"You want to join us, podner?" he'd say.

"Thanks, but I'm a pirate," I'd answer.

"Well, good luck then."

"Thanks."

And they would be gone in a cloud of dust and good feeling.

It turned out to be nothing like that at all. It was the middle of the night when the Texas Chief streamliner crossed over a river from Oklahoma into Texas. I couldn't see anything out of the train window except the reflection of a yellow moon on the river like from a big flashlight with Eveready batteries. Nothing happened and nobody paid any attention to the coming of Texas except me. Everybody else in the car was asleep.

It wasn't long afterward that I went to sleep, too. Running away to Texas had worn me out.

We were in Fort Worth, Texas, when I woke up to see a guy sitting in the seat across from me. I was facing the direction the train was going, he was facing back the other way. He looked special. Like a quick-move shortstop. He was about my age, maybe a little older, dressed in a dark blue suit with a stripe in it like furniture-store salesmen wear. The suit was wrinkled and so was his white shirt and the bright red tie. He had on a hat that was shiny white straw. He was sitting down so I couldn't tell if he was short or tall, big or small.

I could definitely tell it had been a while since he had bathed either his body or his belongings.

"Where you headed?" I asked him.

"Galveston."

"Me too. Want to ride along together?"

He looked at me like I was a lunatic. "That's what we're doing, isn't it?"

"Yes, sir."

He wasn't paying much attention to me because he kept looking up and down the aisle as if he was waiting for somebody else to come. He didn't want to talk to me.

"You a Texan?" I asked anyway.

"A what?"

"A Texan. You know, somebody who's from Texas."

"I'm not *from* Texas, I'm *in* Texas. Okay?"

"I'm from Kansas now but soon I will be a Texan, too. . . ."

A look of terror came to his face. He stood up like a shot and raced down the aisle toward the end of the car. He almost ran and I noticed then that he was definitely shorter and smaller than me. Shortstop size.

Then I heard the voice of the conductor coming from the other end, saying, "Tickets, please, tickets, please," and I knew what the deal was. The conductor was squat like a catcher, like Uncle Bill Mellon, my dad's younger brother who drove a Steffen's Dairy route truck out of Hutchinson. But his face was round and pockmarked like the one on my mother's second cousin Elmer, who was a telephone man in Osawatomie, which is up by Kansas City.

The conductor looked up at the receipt stub stuck up on the baggage rack over my head and then at the seat across from me. There was a beat-up leather satchel bag on it that belonged to the shortstop guy in the straw hat and rumpled suit.

"Somebody sitting there?" said the conductor in a voice that was a lot like my dad's.

"No, sir. That's my bag," said I.

"Didn't I see somebody in a straw hat there a while ago?"

"No, sir. Must not have."

He walked on and that was that. I had just told my first major lie to a major person like a train conductor. Up until then I almost always told the truth to everybody but particularly to grownups. It was part of my training to be a Kansas

State Highway Patrolman and a man of the law. "Somebody sitting there?" said the conductor in a voice that was a lot like my dad's. "No, sir, that's my bag," said I in a voice that was a lot like a pirate captain's, I was sure.

Whatever happened to that trooper's kid who lost his eye in that kick-the-can game?

I hear he ran away to be a pirate and lied to the conductor on the Texas Chief streamliner.

The shortstop guy came back a few minutes later. Now he was ready to be my best and most grateful friend.

"What can I do for you? Name it. Just name it," he said.

"There's nothing. It's all in a life's day."

"The conductor would have thrown me off this train and had me arrested maybe. What's your name?" He stuck his right hand across to me.

I had been working on the answer to that question for a while and now the first time to try it was finally there.

"The One-Eyed Mack," I said.

"Mac? Your name is Mac?"

"The One-Eyed Mack is my name."

"Mac, as in Gil MacDougald?"

"Mack as in truck."

"Yeah, yeah. Have it your way. I'm just trying to be polite because of what you did."

"What's your name?"

"Tom Bell Bowen. Call me Pepper."

"Pepper? That's the name of my dad's sergeant's dog back in Kansas."

"I ain't no dog. It comes from the Bell. My second-grade teacher stuck 'Pepper' after it and everybody picked it up."

"I don't get it."

"Bell pepper. You never eaten a bell pepper?"

"I guess not."

"Your dad in the army?"

"No, is yours?"

"You said something about his sergeant."

"He's a Kansas state trooper."

"Great. Just what I need."

"Don't worry about him bothering you down here in Texas. He's mainly interested in catching speeders anyhow."

"What are you up to in Galveston?"

"I'm going to be a pirate."

"That explains the getup."

"What?"

"The eyepatch and the hat business."

I pulled the patch up off the socket so he could see what wasn't under it. "The patch is because I lost my eye."

"And the hat is because you lost your mind?"

He smiled, so I smiled, even though I didn't think that was very funny.

The guy had a stickiness to him. The same kind you get on your fingers after eating a Milky Way in the summertime. Milky Way was my favorite candy bar so it wasn't all bad. He also seemed pretty smart. Smarter than me, for sure. Wearing a blue suit and a white shirt, even though they were both dirty and wrinkled, was a good clue that he might have gone to college for four years instead of just two. I liked his voice, too. It was soft and twangy and reminded me of how Roy Rogers, the King of the Cowboys, sounded on KFH Radio, Wichita.

"What will you be doing in Galveston?" I tried to talk

twangy but my voice cracked and it didn't work.

But he ignored it and just answered, "Write obits like usual."

"Obits?"

"Obituaries. Stories about dead people."

"Write for who?"

"The Galveston newspaper, if they'll hire me."

"You know how?"

"How what?"

"To write stories about dead people?"

"That's what I do."

"Is it hard?"

"Naw. They're all the same except for names of the people and the funeral home and the cause of death, when the family will let you say what it is."

"Why wouldn't the family want people to know that?"

"Got me." He scooted over more toward the window and put his head against it. "I think I'll catch a wink. Okay?"

"Why did you leave Fort Worth?"

His eyes were closed but I knew he wasn't sleepy. He just didn't want to talk to me anymore. No more gratitude talk. But I figured nuts to him because I was going to need somebody to eat a meal with in Galveston and he was better than nobody.

"Why did you leave Fort Worth? I said."

He opened his eyes like it was the hardest thing he had ever done in his life. "I got in a poker game with the governor of Texas and the mayor of Fort Worth and Ted Williams and lost all track of time, and when it was over I had missed two days of work and my job was gone. Anything else?" He closed his eyes again.

"All I believe is that they fired you."

"Believe all or none."

"I've never known anybody who was fired."

"Well, I've never known anybody who didn't have a left eye. Okay?"

The guy was a sap. I had made a mistake in telling my first major lie to a major person to help him out. Most shortstops, except for Pee Wee Reese of the Dodgers, were the same way. Their mouths worked faster than their brains.

I wasn't about to shut up.

"You must have lost everything in that poker game or wherever, because you sure don't look like you have much."

Both eyes were opened now. He moved his head slightly off the window. I continued:

"I figured it from your awful smell and clothes. It's a wonder the conductor didn't pick up your awful stink from up the line in Oklahoma City and keep you off the train in the first place."

"I'm sorry about what I said about the eye. Okay?" he said.

"Then I'm sorry about what I said about your stink. Okay?"

He was back sitting up straight now. "How old are you anyhow?"

"Almost twenty. You?

"Twenty-three and two-thirds."

"You ever been to Galveston before?"

"Nope. You?"

"Nope."

"Where have you been?"

"Wichita, Newton and Hutchinson mostly, and other places in Kansas. How about you?"

"All over Kansas and Oklahoma and Texas. If it's big enough to have a bank I've been there."

"Bank? I thought you wrote about dead people. My sister works for a bank in Kansas."

"I like to go in and watch them count their money."

"You want to be a pirate with me?"

"No thank you."

"You did pretty good with the conductor. Where did you hide anyway?"

"Up on top of the commode tank in the ladies'."

"The ladies'?"

"I told the ladies who came in I was fixing something and to come back, and the conductor just knocked on the door and there was no answer."

"You'd be a fine pirate, it sounds like to me."

"Maybe in the next life."

"You believe there's more than one."

"I don't believe it, I just hope it. It goes with being a Holy Road."

"We're Methodists but I played on the same high school team with a Holy Road. He was our centerfielder. Fast on the takeoff for a fly ball. Really fast."

"Well, hooray."

"Yeah. Hooray."

I went out of the car first and Pepper was right behind me. But on the station platform I turned around to say something about how much I liked the looks of the Galveston train station. He wasn't there. Tom Bell Pepper Bowen had disappeared.

Good-bye to you, too, you lousy stinking Holy Road little writer about dead people!

The station was huge and noisy and fancy. It was crowded with black and white people with a lot of suitcases and chil-

dren and boxes. Everybody and everything seemed hot and
wet. Particularly me. I had never been that hot in April in
my Kansas life. I was suddenly wet under my arms and across
my back and under my hat and in my crotch and seat. How
can I be a pirate if I'm drowning in my sweat all the time?

Outside wasn't much better. I looked to the left and there
was a monstrous warehouse, to the right the Salvation Army
and some houses. Straight ahead was where the tall buildings
seemed to be, so straight ahead it was. There were even more
people on the sidewalks, most of them wearing very few
clothes for April and all of them paying no attention to me.
Maybe they were just used to seeing young men from Kansas
with patches over their left eye, wearing old Kansas State
Highway Patrolmen's hats with the brim pinned up and back.

I hadn't gone two blocks when I wanted to cry. There was
nobody in this place I could eat a tunafish-salad sandwich
and drink a Grapette with. Nobody who knew me well enough
to like me, well enough to care if I fell under the tracks of
the Texas Chief streamliner or if a tree fell on me. I hated
it that I wanted to cry. Some pirate I was going to be. Give
me your watch and your money, Mr. Rich Man, or I'll cry.

*Whatever happened to the trooper's kid who lost his eye and
went off to Texas to be a pirate?*

He got off the train and cried.

Maybe I'll be a pirate some other time. Maybe I'll just go
right on back home to Kansas and keep mowing and sickling
for the county awhile longer. I had a good train ride down
and Tom Bell Pepper Bowen was kind of fun to meet, even
if he was a lousy stinking Holy Road little writer of stories
about dead people who ditched me. Dad and Meg were probably crazy with worry now. Dad probably sent out a missing-
persons on me and had all the depots and hospitals and

morgues and police stations all over Kansas checked for me. I guessed Meg had been crying since about six o'clock Friday when they figured out I wasn't coming home for dinner and was gone on the 1:22 doodle bug train. Maybe gone forever even.

What I really needed was something to eat. Not just anything. I had to have a tuna sandwich and a Grapette and that was that. There was a Rexall right there on the corner when it hit me, and they had a sign that said "Fountain Service."

No tuna left, said the lady behind the counter. She was nice about it. Reminded me a lot of Mrs. Andrews, mother of Lisa Andrews, the head cheerleader and Miss Posture Perfect who laughed at my body parts in the dream. The lady said to try the depot café at the train station. I told her thank you. But there was no way I was going back to the train station right then.

I kept walking toward the tall buildings. Here I was, in Galveston, Texas. I should have asked the librarian how big it was. I didn't think it was a big city like Wichita or Kansas City. But it was. Where were the ocean and the boats? It didn't matter really because now I was just going to get a bite to eat and go home, but it would be too bad if I left without seeing any water or boats.

I saw a sign for a cafeteria in the next block. Luby's Cafeteria. "Continuous Serving All Day Long." There were no other customers except for an old man who looked scroungy enough in dirty and wrinkled clothes to be Tom Bell Pepper Bowen's father. He was off in a corner drinking what looked like a cup of coffee. He probably put a lot of sugar and cream in it like my grandfather on Momma's side did.

They had tuna sandwiches right there, already made up, with several other kinds of sandwiches.

"Does the tuna salad have egg in it?" I asked the lady behind the counter. I hated egg in my tunafish-salad sandwiches.

"Whoever heard of putting egg in tuna salad?"

"They do that a lot in Kansas."

"This ain't Kansas, is it?"

"No, ma'am."

I took the sandwich down to the drink section on a tray. She went along with me on the other side of the cafeteria counter.

"You have Grapette?"

"You'll see it there."

Sure enough. I saw it there. I took the bottle and put it on my tray.

"Don't you want it opened?"

"Yes, ma'am. It'd be hard to drink it with the lid still on."

She came close to smiling. Maybe I dreamed it.

"Watch the fizz," I said.

"Grapettes don't fizz like Coca-Colas," she said.

I knew that.

She opened the Grapette and gave it back to me. And we both went on to the cash register at the end of the serving line.

"Will there be anything else?" she asked, as if she didn't really expect there to be, because she was looking down at my tray and ringing up my tuna sandwich and Grapette.

Yes, as a matter of fact, I'd also like eighty-four hamburgers with pickles and mustard. Hold the onions on thirty-two of them, fry the onions on twelve and put them on raw on every third one of the rest, unless you have Velveeta for them. And to go with them please make up sixty-two Cokes, forty-one Dr Peppers, twenty-two Grapettes. . . .

"That'll be a dollar seven."

"Seven?"

"Seven cents. One dollar and seven cents."

"Yes, ma'am."

I paid and took my eats over to the corner farthest away from the man who could be Tom Bell Pepper Bowen's relative.

The sandwich was awful. You would have thought with their own ocean right here they could have made tuna into a good tuna sandwich. But there was too much mayonnaise and not enough of everything else. But the Grapette was wonderful and perfect. It was cold and I drank it right out of the bottle. The only problem with Grapettes was, they were smaller than most every other kind of soda pop, which meant you had to go slow or it was gone before the food.

It was the first time I had eaten by myself in a restaurant. I didn't like it at all. I wanted to talk to somebody, to tell them how bad the tuna sandwich was compared to the ones back home and how great the Grapette was and how I had decided not to be a pirate right now after all.

A young Mexican kid in an apron was sweeping the floor of the place. I decided to guess how long it would take him to get over where I was. Five minutes and thirty-nine seconds was my official guess. It was over seven minutes and I was through with the sandwich and had only two sips of the Grapette left when he got there. He was sixteen or seventeen years old. His hair was slicked back with some kind of grease and his fingernails were dirty, but he seemed nice enough. I had never talked to a Mexican before.

"You looking for a girl?" he said.

"No thank you."

"I will get you one cheap."

"No thank you."

"You don't like it in Galveston? Girls, cards, dice, dope and everything is here. I will help you have a good time."

"No thank you."

He pointed to his left eye. "What happened to you?"

"I lost it in the war."

"There ain't no wars now. You too young for the others."

"It was the Mexican war."

"There ain't no Mexican war."

"You from Mexico?"

"Not me. I from Port Arthur."

"Then you don't know about Mexican wars, do you?"

"Why you wear that hat?"

"Because my head is cold."

"You crazy man."

He moved on with his broom.

It was an awful life I was leading.

3

The Beaumont Rocket

There in front of me down the street, like a magic gift from Thunderbird heaven, was the Galveston bus depot. Why not go back to Kansas on the bus? One trip on the Texas Chief streamliner was enough for each life.

Junior Dillard wouldn't get any of the money here in Galveston. It was even a different bus line.

The Texas Red Rocket Motor Bus Company.

There at the first loading-dock slot was a bus with its motor running, like it was really anxious to get a move on. BEAUMONT ROCKET, it said on the destination sign. Two or three people, including a woman in a purple and yellow dress with long blond hair, were standing at the bus door waiting to get on. It was a strange-looking bus, smaller than a Thunderbird. It had an air scoop up top in back that looked like an upside-down comma. On the front under the windshield it said FLXIBLE. What happened to the first E? I decided it must have been named after the guy who invented the bus, like the phones were named for Alexander Graham Bell.

Hi there. I'd like to introduce you to my uncle and aunt from Ohio, Rob and Mary Flxible. Uncle Rob invented the bus with the air scoop on the back that looks like an upside-down comma.

The agent inside behind the ticket counter was about Pepper's age, only his hair was short and his voice was squeaky like my sister Meg's. He was a rightfielder type who did not strike me as being very good at making out tickets or doing all of the other things a ticket agent must do. But he did have two eyes. What's the matter, friend, afraid to go outside and watch a kick-the-can game?

"Where is Beaumont?" He repeated my question like it was something that should go into a museum of the most stupid things ever asked at the Texas Red Rocket Motor Bus Company bus depot, Galveston, Texas.

"It's east of here," he answered.

"On the way to Kansas?"

"Not as much as Houston is."

"When's the next bus to Houston?"

"You just missed one. The next one's in an hour and fifteen minutes."

"How much to Beaumont?"

"Two dollars and one cent with tax."

"I'll take it without, thank you."

"Without what?"

"The tax."

He cracked a slight, ever so slight smile and reached behind him to the card ticket case, pulled out a two-piece card ticket and stamped it on the back with a validator. I gave him two one-dollar bills and a penny.

"Next!" he yelled, like he was calling the roll at the penitentiary. Next for solitary confinement. Next for the electric chair.

Next to have your left eye cut out with a tin-can lid. Next not to be hired by The Thunderbird. Next to be ditched by a smelly little Holy Road named Tom Bell Pepper Bowen. Next to cry.

There were only three other passengers. The lady with the purple and yellow dress and long blond hair, a Mexican like the kid in the cafeteria, only older, and a regular-looking man in a sport coat with no tie. They were all sitting in separate seats from the middle of the bus to the front and I took a seat in the back. When I walked down the aisle to it, I passed the lady and she smiled at me like we were old friends. She was at least thirty years old.

The driver, short, pot-bellied and full of chatter like a third-base coach, reminded me a lot of Dad's friend who drove for The Thunderbird. He closed the door and stood by his seat up front and faced us, his loyal passengers.

"Our running time to Beaumont on this magnificent little Rocket is two hours and fifty minutes. Please sit back and enjoy yourself. If I can do anything to help you I'll be right up here behind this wheel. You can't miss me. Thank you."

He sat down, threw the bus in reverse and started to pull away from the loading dock. But then he stopped. One last passenger came running up and on. It was Pepper. *The* Pepper. Tom Bell Pepper Bowen, the stinky little Holy Road writer about dead people himself!

I hoped he had a ticket because there sure wasn't a ladies' room on this bus for him to hide in.

He didn't see me. He didn't even look toward the back of

the bus, and just took a seat near the front. The same dirty, wrinkled clothes and white straw hat were on him. I thought about going up there and sitting down next to him and saying: "Hi, I'm The One-Eyed Mack from the Federal Bureau of Investigation. J. Edgar Hoover personally ordered me aboard this Beaumont Rocket to arrest you, Tom Bell Pepper Bowen, for stealing a ride on the Texas Chief from Fort Worth, Texas, to Galveston, Texas. If you will just come quietly now, I will tie you down on a Sante Fe Railroad track so your head can be cut off. Thank you."

The first thing our wonderful little Rocket did was get on a ferry for a ride across a big bay to a place where there was a lighthouse, a ferry station and the beginning of the road to Beaumont. It had begun to rain a little so nobody got out of the bus on the ferry. The driver said we could if we wanted to, as long as we were back on the bus once we got to the other side, which he called Bolivar Point. It was only a fifteen-minute ride. I decided I wouldn't get out no matter what, because Pepper might see me. Who needs him? I can eat tuna sandwiches and drink Grapettes by myself.

I was on the right side of the bus, the ocean side. At first there wasn't that much to see. Mostly sand and little beach houses and little bushes and rocks and a few people. But after a while there was the ocean, the Gulf of Mexico, right outside the window as we zipped along. At least I saw some water. There were a few fishing boats out but I didn't see any pirates on any of them.

Why not go up there and talk to Pepper? What can he do except scream like a crazy person until I go away? But why do I want to talk to a lousy stinking little Holy Road who ditched me at the train station?

I walked up there and sat down by him. His eyes were

closed but it didn't look to me he was that asleep.

"Hey, there are plenty of empty seats," he kind of muttered as I sat down. Then he saw who it was and straightened up. I thought he might smile but he didn't. He still didn't like me and that was that.

"Hi, I'm The One-Eyed Mack with the Sante Fe Railroad police and I'm here to arrest you for stealing a ride on the Texas Chief streamliner. If you'll just come with me, I'll arrange to have you drowned in the ladies'-room commode on our next train north. Thank you."

"What are you doing going to Beaumont?"

"I have pirate business there."

"Look, I'm sorry we lost each other at the train station. It sure was crowded, wasn't it?"

"Sure was. I thought you were going to write dead-people stories in Galveston."

"They wouldn't hire me."

"How did you get two dollars and one penny including tax for a ticket to Beaumont?"

"I found it."

"Where?"

"Under my pillow."

"You going to stay in Beaumont or just passing through?"

"Staying. The guy at the Galveston paper said he knew they were looking for bodies at the Beaumont paper."

"Dead bodies to write about?"

"Live bodies to write about dead bodies."

"Good luck, then."

"You going to be a pirate in Beaumont?"

"Maybe."

"Maybe we can hang a couple when we get there."

"Hang a couple of what?"

"Drinks. What's your favorite pleasure?"

"Grapette. I just had one back at a cafeteria in Galveston by myself with a tuna sandwich."

"Good." He moved his head back against the window again like he was going to try to sleep again. "How about we both try to get some rest so we can really do it right in Beaumont. Okay?"

"Okay." I got up and started back toward the back. I had one last question. "Where did you really find that money?"

"I got it from a rich man who didn't need it as much as I did."

"What rich man?"

"You going to turn me into the Kansas Highway Patrol?"

"What rich man?"

"The conductor on the Texas Chief."

"How did you do that?"

"I told him my left eye was about to fall out and I needed two dollars and one cent to buy a new one."

I headed back toward my seat feeling like a fresh fried chicken. My grandmother on my momma's side used to warn me to stay away from the stove when she was frying chicken. "The splatters will burn your soul," she said.

Tom Bell Pepper Bowen burned my soul.

Then I had an experience with the blonde lady in the purple and yellow dress.

She gave me a giant wink when I went by her on the way back to my seat. Without really thinking it through, I winked back just as big. I sat down again and there she was, right there with me. She sat down next to me. Up close she looked older than I thought. She may have been as old as thirty-five, in fact. But she had a smooth complexion like the women in the Breck's shampoo magazine ads. Her lips were caked with lipstick and her cheeks were caked with rouge and the rest of her was caked with perfume and powder. Her dress was cut way down in the front and there was no way to even look at her without seeing more of her bosoms than a one-eyed stranger on a bus should be allowed to see.

She talked like she had known me all her life, like we had been Hatchets together at Carrie Nation High or something. Before long she had her right hand on my left knee. We just went on talking about how Stan the Man could slice it to right when he had to and how Kansas is known for its Turkey-red wheat and how it rained in Galveston every afternoon and how the Gulf of Mexico wasn't a real ocean and how her name was Lillian and I called myself The One-Eyed Mack.

Before long, just as I was beginning to tell her about the awful tuna sandwich and the wonderful Grapette I'd had in the cafeteria, she moved her hand right up inside my leg. I could feel the top side of her hand against my most vital part.

"Do you want to have some fun, One-Eyed Mack?" she inquired.

"Sure," I replied.

This was the kind of experience all of us in Kansas dreamed about. There you are, minding your own business, when an older woman demands you for her very own. Just like that. Usually the woman was a schoolteacher or a radio singer. That did not figure to be the case with Lillian but otherwise it was right out of the book.

"Sure," I said again.

The next thing I knew she unbuttoned the fly of my dark blue corduroys.

And the next thing I knew after that, I was coming. Like

the Arkansas River out of its banks, I was coming. It flowed all over my undershorts and down my right leg and blue corduroy pants into my sock and shoe.

Lillian only smiled and with her left hand pulled several paper towels and Kleenexes out of her purse and cleaned it and me all up. Like it was nothing. Like it happened all the time. Like, what else is new?

"That'll be three dollars, dear heart," she said, once things were tidied up.

"For what?" I could not believe it!

"For the come, dear boy. That's the standard rate."

"But we didn't . . . you know, really do anything."

"That's not my fault, is it?" Her voice was stone, like a teacher you've just told you didn't get the homework done because lightning struck your house and burned up your belongings and your family. "The standard hand rate, white on white, is three dollars."

"Standard where?"

"Galveston, dear one."

"I'm from Kansas."

"I'm from Galveston. Pay me three or I start yelling that you stuck your hand down the front of my dress."

"Nobody'd care."

"The driver would, dear heart. He's my husband."

I took three dollars out of my pocket and gave them to her as fast as my hands would move.

She stood up in the aisle.

"Sorry about the eye, dearie," she said, like she was the school nurse.

"I poked it out intentionally myself."

"Well, have a good time in Beaumont or wherever your

star finally takes you," she said. "You're a dear boy."

She went back up front.

I had a problem. The front of my blue corduroys was soaked. I opened the bus window there by me and got up on my knees in the seat. Then by leaning back like Roger the Rubberman at the Sorghum Festival I held my wet front up to the open window. The rain was gone and the air was warm. It worked to dry them out and I felt smart.

After a while we came to a town the driver hollered out as High Island. The bus stopped at a little grocery store and the driver got out and went inside. When he got back on the bus, he walked straight back to me.

I thought Lillian the Come Lady must have told him what happened and now I would be killed.

Whatever happened to the trooper's one-eyed kid who ran off to be a pirate?

He came in his pants on The Beaumont Rocket and the driver beat him to death with his ticket punch.

"I've been watching you in the rearview mirror, son," he said in a low voice, for which I was grateful. "Don't expose yourself like that out the window. There could be small children playing out there."

"Yes, sir."

"Exposing yourself to innocent people is against the law in Texas."

"Yes, sir. Thank you."

He had one question before resuming his duties behind the wheel of The Beaumont Rocket.

"What happened to the eye?"

"Stan Musial took it."

"Okay. Sorry. Just behave yourself."

41

"Yes, sir." I had one question for him. "Are you related to the woman up there in the purple and yellow dress?"

He frowned. "That kind of smart talk will get you thrown right off this bus."

It really was an awful life I was living.

4

Hanging a Grapette

I was sure the little Bell Pepper didn't plan to hang a drink or anything else with me in Beaumont. He was going to ditch his one-eyed nuisance as soon as he could, just like what happened in Galveston. But I decided to make it really hard for him. Why not have some mean fun before going back to the mowing and the sickling?

So when The Beaumont Rocket got into the outskirts of what I knew was Beaumont from the road signs, I moved up to his seat and sat down by him. My front was almost completely dry and it didn't seem to me there was much of a smell left. As awful as he stank he couldn't have picked up a whiff of the world's largest garbage dump.

He frowned. I smiled. He grunted. I smiled. Oh, it was so clear from his lousy stinking Holy Road face that he wished I was somewhere else.

Glue, little Bell Pepper! Glue! I am sticking to you like you are a model Messerschmidt and I am a tube of airplane glue!

I got up and let him get off the bus in front of me. Inside, he said he needed to go to the bathroom. He said he had to go badly and it might take him a while, if I knew what he meant. I knew what he meant all right, and I went in there with him and took the stall next to him even though I couldn't do anything in there except sit.

He got through. I got through. He washed his hands at a sink. I washed mine at the one next to it.

"Let's go see what this town's got for us," he said.

"Let's do," I said.

Shake me if you can, little Bell Pepper!

We went outside and walked a block before going into a place called D.B.'s Sabine Bar and Grill. He hung a Jax beer and a dime pack of salted peanuts and I hung a Grapette and a nickel sack of Fritos. I paid for it all. He didn't say three words to me the whole time. I spent most of the time looking across him at a big Budweiser painted picture on the wall of General Custer's last battle with the Indians.

Then we went into a department store called The White House that reminded me of Roebaugh-Buck's in Wichita. It was his idea to go in but he never said what we were doing in there other than just walking around. He was hoping and looking for a chance to make a run for it.

Finally he took a pair of dark charcoal-gray slacks to try on. A saleslady about the age and size of my tiny Aunt Wilma in Chanute did everything but cry and hold her nose as he walked off toward one of those little fitting booths they have in fancy stores. I went with him and stood right outside the curtain.

"I didn't know you liked charcoal gray," I said in a loud voice through the curtain.

"There's a lot you don't know."

"I'm learning."

No answer.

It was wonderful.

He came back out and handed the pants back to the woman. "They don't fit," he said.

She was holding a handkerchief to her nose and mouth. I am sure she took those pants and threw them in an incinerator after we left.

Back out on the sidewalk the little Bell Pepper said we had pretty much seen Beaumont, so why didn't he go over and see about the dead-bodies job at the newspaper?

"You do what you have to do and we'll meet up and hang another drink or two later," he said.

"I don't have a thing on my schedule right now," I said. "I'll go with you."

He looked at me like he'd gladly have taken a tin-can lid and torn out my other eye.

Walking next to him made me feel good. He was about five-eight and since I was five-ten that meant he had to look up at me when we talked.

Also, I was kind of liking him. He had a lot of life and spunk for a liar who was so small and smelly.

The newspaper office was one very cruddy place. It looked like it had never really been painted on the inside. There were worn-out chairs in the lobby, and whoever was in charge of sweeping out and emptying the trashcans needed to be jacked or fired. The bus station didn't smell any worse. I hadn't realized how awful the working conditions were for people who wrote about dead people in the newspapers.

Pepper said for me to wait there in the lobby while he found out where to go. He kind of waved to me as he disappeared up some ratty steps and I figured that was that for Tom Bell Pepper Bowen. I'd never see him again. Not in this life. But I decided to sit down and wait awhile anyhow. Why not give the stinking little Holy Road a chance to do right?

There was a copy of the newspaper there on one of the chairs. It was yesterday's and part of the front page was gone. I didn't care because I didn't care about the news. Dad used to read the paper a lot and so did Mom once in a while on weekends. But it wasn't for me. Except the sports section and then mostly in the summer during the baseball season so I could follow the Cardinals and the National League. Our paper printed all the National box scores and always ran long stories about the Kansas and national semi-pro championships at Lawrence Stadium in Wichita. During the war, Jimmy T.'s daddy took him to Wichita to see Pistol Pete Reiser of the Dodgers play in a semi-pro game for the Fort Riley Army Base team and Pistol Pete went three for four.

I sometimes read the sports section during the football season, to follow the colleges. I liked Doak Walker, who played for SMU in Texas. He was quick and little and kicked and ran and passed and was everything most everybody I knew wished they were. Including me, except when I wanted to be Stan the Man or a state trooper.

But the rest of the newspaper never made any sense. Why read all of those long stories about people I'd never heard of doing things to others they shouldn't be doing?

Why should I care? I lost my left eye and Junior Dillard wouldn't hire me and I came in my pants on The Beaumont Rocket and here I am in a place called Beaumont with a stinky little Holy Road named Tom Bell Pepper Bowen who has probably just ditched me again.

I grabbed my white Roebaugh-Buck's bag and went up the stairs. One floor up, there was a big open room with a dozen or so rundown desks with people smoking cigarettes behind them. Some were also typing on typewriters, talking on the phone or reading newspapers.

I went over to the first desk to a man with a gray felt hat and a dark brown suit coat on. He was heavy-chested like a leftfielder.

"I'm looking for a guy in a straw hat, carrying a suitcase," I said to him.

"Look to your heart's content," he said, waving his right hand like he was introducing some act on stage.

"His name is Bowen and he came up here to get a job."

"What job?"

"Writing about dead people."

"Obits, you mean?"

"Yes, sir."

"Couldn't be here. We only have one person doing that and she's still alive herself." He turned around to the room and yelled, "Hey, George! That kid who was up here a while ago. Did he apply for a job?"

George yelled back: "The guy in the blue suit and the white straw hat?"

"That's the one."

"He just wanted to know the way out."

The man in the hat then pointed me toward the rear door and I took a step that way.

"Hey, kid," he said. "What happened to the eye?"

"Doak Walker tore it out."

"Where did you play against the Doaker?"

"He's my brother."

"Is that right? What's your name?"

"Roper Walker."

"What does the hat mean?"

"It means I'm the Doaker's brother and he tore my eye out."

Telling lies to adults was getting easier and easier.

The back steps led to an alley behind the newspaper building and that alley was a mess of old newspapers and boxes and junk and garbage and cats and dogs and drunk men in undershirts. A couple of the men smiled and asked me for money and the others just smiled. I could see me ending up like them.

Whatever happened to the trooper's kid who lost his eye in the kick-the-can game?

He came in his pants on The Beaumont Rocket and lives in his undershirt behind the newspaper in Beaumont, Texas.

It was almost dark and the question was, what now, One-Eyed Mack? Back to the bus station and on to Kansas? Or find some place to spend the night and go off in the morning?

At the end of the alley I turned right and there in the next block, like a magic answer from heaven, I saw a tiny neon sign. In red it said, "Magnolia House Hotel. Rooms."

I had stayed in a hotel only once in my life. We had gone to Chanute for the funeral of an uncle and an incredible snowstorm blew in from Nebraska and marooned everyone. There wasn't enough room in family houses for us to spend the night so Momma, Dad, Meg and I took a room at the Hotel Chanute. It was a red brick building with an elevator and the constant noise of trains going by. Meg said she was afraid passengers on the trains could see in our window, but other than that and the smell of Lifebuoy soap and Lysol in the bathroom I didn't remember anything else.

I had never eaten a meal alone in a restaurant until Luby's Cafeteria in Galveston. I had never stayed in a hotel alone until now and the Magnolia House in Beaumont.

The room had a smell of mothballs and a single bed with a white and red rosebud bedspread on it. There was a chest of drawers with a mirror over it, an overhead light in the middle of the room and a sink with running water.

The bathroom was down the hall and it had a commode and a bathtub. I wasn't about to use them if I could help it. I hated to take a bath or go to the bathroom away from home. I know it's something I should have thought about more before I got on the 1:22 Sante Fe doodle bug. Avoiding the bath was not a big problem but the other was. When I was ten years old I went six straight days without moving my bowels. We were at my Aunt Mary's house in Coffeyville and the bathroom was right next to where my grandmother was sick with the flu. I was afraid she wouldn't like my sounds and I would have been embarrassed to see her afterward.

Who was that in the bathroom from 8:07 to 8:17 last night?
It was me, Grandmother.
Your noises kept me awake, son.
Sorry, Grandmother.

I spent no more than four or five minutes thinking about Tom Bell Pepper Bowen before falling off to sleep. I wondered where the stinking little Holy Road jerk was resting his filthy, lying, rotten head this night.

I wondered what in the world he really was besides a liar.

The Magnolia House had no coffee shop or café. A goofy-looking man at the desk suggested a place around the corner for breakfast. He said it was called The Hut and it was close, clean and cheap. I liked the guy because he didn't ask me about my eye or hat. That was probably because he knew he was stranger-looking than me. His head was larger than most and it was shaved clean all over and was white like Meg's patent-leather white majorette's boots. He had two eyes but they were tiny and dark blue, like the marks Rand McNally used for towns in the road atlas I saw at the library. He never stood up so I had no idea of how big he was. I guessed at least six feet. Maybe seven or maybe even ten. Who knows? His voice was a low gurgle and reminded me of Coach Davidson's when he was playing around talking into a Coca-Cola bottle.

The only thing I ever collected was Coca-Cola bottles. I picked them up for the names of the towns they had on the bottom. I had twenty-three different ones when I finally decided I was too old for that anymore and took them to the A&P for the money. The farthest-away bottle I had said Mobile, Alabama, on the bottom. It made me want to go to Mobile, Alabama.

I went to The Hut. It was not a hut. It was a place in the middle of the block that was about as wide as a car and had only one row of stools and a counter. One man in a white hat and apron behind the counter did everything. He took the orders, cooked them, served them, collected the money and cleaned up. He was like a centerfielder who also ran in and played short and pitched, too. And he did it all without saying a word to anybody.

I wanted an egg over easy with bacon and toast and a small glass of grapefruit juice. I told him. He wrote it down and went over and got it working on the griddle. Then he dished up two previous orders that were ready, cleaned away dirty dishes at a stool position, took some money from another customer, dried off some clean wet plates and poured somebody a second cup of coffee. I had never seen anything like him.

"Hey, sir," I said when he delivered my order. "Do you want me to give you a hand back there?"

The guy, who was about thirty-five years old, did not stop or say a word. It was like he didn't hear me.

"Really, I'd be glad to help. Not for pay or anything," I said after him.

The man on the stool next to me said, "Leave him alone. Billy here can't talk. The Japs cut his tongue out."

"I didn't know that."

"You would have thought a guy with only one eye would know that. You of all people."

"Sure."

Sure. All of us cripples have our own signs, our own language, our own sounds like dogs that nobody but us cripples understands. I see a guy with only one leg, one arm, no hair, three feet, two fingers, and we are brothers.

If I was established as The One-Eyed Mack, feared pirate and adventurer, I would see to it that the knife I have here to butter my toast ends up blade-first in the middle of your Adam's apple!

"He's the best short-order man in North America," the man said.

"No, he isn't. Pepper Bell is better."

"Never heard of him."

"Works at a place called Cokes in Mobile, Alabama."

He went back to eating his breakfast and so did I.

I started thinking about how I might use him in an experiment. A pirate experiment. I might as well try being a pirate just once before I retired, was the way I was figuring as I ate the egg and the bacon and sipped at the grapefruit juice.

Without moving anything but my good right eye I looked him over. Brown work clothes with the name "Bud" embroidered over one pocket, "Courtesy Plumbing Inc." on the other. A plumber. I liked plumbers or at least I liked the only one I ever knew who came to fix our commode once and unclog the outside drain from the kitchen sink another time. Maybe Kansas plumbers were different from those in Texas. This one looked old, about thirty, and he looked like he played football in high school, but not baseball because he wasn't smart enough. He looked married but probably to a woman who dreaded him coming home every night because he smelled like sewers and septic tanks and broken commodes. I decided she'd leave him in a minute if the right chance presented itself in the form of a handsome man in a cleaner line of work. Maybe the pirate thing for me to do was find that handsome man in a cleaner line of work for her. That would be a little like giving to the poor.

I timed the final bites of my food so I would be through eating about the same time he was. I paid the man with no tongue eighty-seven cents and got outside just before Bud the Plumber did. I stood at the curb casually, like I was looking for something, and watched him get in his truck, which was a green and white International pickup with "Courtesy Plumbing Inc." written all over it. There was a phone number. 3427. I memorized it. There was an address. 128 South Gilpen. I memorized that. But then the truck and Bud the Plumber drove away and there I was, still standing there casually. Now what?

I could call Courtesy Plumbing Inc. and ask to talk to Bud.

When they said he wasn't there I could say I was with the Red Cross and the pint of blood he ordered was in, but it wouldn't keep long so I needed immediately the complete and true spelling of his whole name and his home address and phone number. Then I would go to either the newspaper office or the bus depot, find a handsome man who had a clean job and send him out to Bud's house. I would tell him to tell Bud's wife that he was from Courtesy Plumbing Inc. and that he regretted to inform her that Bud had fallen headfirst into an open septic tank. He did not drown and he was safe but it would probably be weeks, maybe months, before he smelled right again. Courtesy wanted her to be prepared to scrub him down in Lysol and Lux four times a day and to know the company stood behind them both all the way, no matter how long it took to bring him back to normal smell. Then Bud's wife should break into tears and fall into the man's arms for comfort and he should say that the other thing she could do is just go away until the smell goes away. He was then to fall in love with her as they drove away in the car together and she'd do the same and that would be that. A good day's work for a good pirate.

Before long I had my white Roebaugh-Buck's sack in my hand and was on the way to the bus station and back home to Kansas.

The bus depot was a crazy house. People were standing around the ticket counter in a big mess instead of in a line and some were yelling and unhappy. A half-drunk man in a dirty undershirt and greasy yellow cowboy hat told me the ticket agent was new and a fool and didn't really know how to make out tickets and everybody was about to miss their bus and nobody cared or was doing anything about it.

Off to the side of the counter I saw a worried black man in a red cap who I decided had to be a porter. I told him I knew how to make out tickets and baggage checks and would be glad to help out. Thank the Good Lord, he said, because the regular agent who was married to a clerk at The White House department store had run off on the 8:10 to New Orleans with a waitress in the depot café who was married to a Dodge-Plymouth mechanic's helper. The depot manager was on vacation visiting his wife's folks in Amarillo and that left only this kid who had just started and didn't know a bus ticket from a hole in his right ear. He took me around through a back entrance and told the agent help had arrived. The agent, a blond-headed guy in a crew cut, about twenty-two or twenty-three, looked at my hat and my eyepatch and probably was thinking, No thanks. But I guess the noise and the confusion and the angry people caused him to say, Sure. Like me, he was too old to cry, but also like me he sure looked like he wanted to.

In ten minutes the Crew Cut was ready to give me the Congressional Medal of Honor and elect me Stan the Man or anything else I wanted to be. I quickly had people who were waiting for the Liberty–Dayton–Houston and the Vidor–Orange–Lake Charles–Lafayette–New Orleans Greyhounds get in one line while those for the Texas Red Rocket Motor Bus Company and the other smaller lines got in another. I told Crew Cut to take care of the Greyhounds and I would do the rest. We zipped through them and I was a hero.

Who was that eyepatched man in the pirate hat who saved the bus depot? He calls himself The One-Eyed Mack.

God bless and keep The One-Eyed Mack!

Then Pepper happened again. There he was, walking into the bus depot like he owned the place. He was wearing that same suit and shirt and hat and carrying that same leather satchel. I was just finishing up a seven-coupon ticket to Worthington, Minnesota. He was already at the ticket counter by the time he spotted me or he might have turned and run. But there he was.

"Hey, sorry about yesterday," he said, without even first saying hello. His clothes were still filthy and he hadn't shaved or bathed and he was a sad case to look at. "They had already filled that job at the newspaper, but they told me about another one that was open at a place behind them but I had to go right then or they'd be closed. Sorry."

"You're lying."

"So what if I am. Give me a ticket."

"Where to?"

"Anywhere, I don't care."

"You serious?"

"What are you doing working here?"

"I'm not working here."

"You're right there behind this ticket counter asking me where I want to buy a ticket to and you look right at me and say you don't work here. Don't preach to me about lying, Mack, or whatever you call yourself."

"The One-Eyed Mack."

"I forgot. How is the pirate business here in Beaumont?"

"How come you don't like me?"

He looked away at the clock on the wall off to the right. "Just give me a ticket to Lufkin."

"Lufkin? What's that?"

"It's a town up the road from here. Look at your maps and things. You'll find it."

I didn't look at any map but I did find a stack of preprinted little card tickets that said, "From Station Stamped on Back to Lufkin, Texas." I stamped it on the back and said, "You got two dollars and fifty-five cents?"

He reached into his pockets and put a couple of handfuls of change on the counter and started counting it out. There were two or three two-bit pieces but most were dimes, nickels and pennies. I could tell he was really embarrassed, even if it was just me.

"It's on the house," I said, pushing his money back toward him.

He smiled like a real human being. I saw his teeth, which were good, and his eyes, which were brown, get wide and watery. "Hey, no, you don't have to do that," he said. "I've got enough here to make it."

"I'm the kind of pirate who takes from the rich and gives to the poor."

"You're not rich."

"The Texas Red Rocket Motor Bus Company is, I bet."

He gave me a wink and said, "Gotcha." He took the ticket off the counter. "Thanks, One-Eyed Mack. Thanks a lot. This is the second time you've given me a hand. I won't forget it. I won't forget it. Neither will He," he said, pointing toward the ratty ceiling of the bus station. It was the first time He had even entered my mind since I left Kansas.

"What are you going to be up to in Lufkin?"

He was in a good mood now. "Oh, I may go back to preaching. Who knows?"

"Preaching? Come on."

He reached across the counter and in a lowered, deep voice said: "The Lord is my savior, I shall not want. He maketh me to lie down in green pastures. He restoreth my soul. My cup runneth over. Surely goodness and mercy shall follow me all the days of my life and I will dwelleth in the House of the Lord forever." He slapped the counter with his right hand. "Amen and Godspeed. There's my bus."

He was through the door to the loading dock in a flash.

I had a quick argument with myself. Should I give Crew Cut two dollars and fifty-five cents for Pepper's ticket? He would never know because he was so busy. But after I was gone he would figure it out. That would mess up everything.

Who was that eyepatched man in the crazy hat?

They call him The One-Eyed Mack.

Well, he just stole a bus ticket to Lufkin, Texas.

Throw the book at him, J. Edgar Hoover!

I yelled over at Crew Cut, "Where is Lufkin?"

"North of here about a hundred miles."

"On the way to Kansas?"

"Kind of, I think."

I took some money out of my pocket. "Here's five ten for two tickets to Lufkin. One for a guy who's already on the bus and the other for me. Okay?"

"Sure, but wait a minute," he said. He was a perfect third-baseman type. "Let me say thank you more than I already have. . . ."

"Haven't time. The bus to Lufkin's leaving." I had my white sack in hand and was out from behind the counter now.

"Who are you?" he yelled after me. "What's your name?"

"They call me The One-Eyed Mack."

"Bless you, One-Eyed Mack. Bless you and keep you."

The Texas Red Rocket to Lufkin was little and had an upside-down-comma air-scoop on its rear like the one from Galveston; it was already moving out the loading-dock driveway toward the street. I ran up to it and beat on its side with a fist and in a few seconds it stopped. I raced up to the door, which the driver opened, and I leaped on.

"Lufkin?" asked the driver.

"Yes, sir," I said, and handed him my ticket.

Tom Bell Pepper Bowen was sitting back about in the middle of the bus. He watched me with a smile as I made my way down the aisle.

I said he watched me with a smile as I made my way down the aisle!

"Is this seat taken?" I asked him when I got to him.

"No, it sure isn't."

I put my white sack in the overhead rack and sat down.

"Where you headed?" Pepper asked.

"Lufkin," I answered.

"Me too. Want to ride along together?" he asked.

"What do you think we're doing?"

It had been a long time since I had been as happy as I was right then.

5
Last Stand

There we were at the Lonesome Pine Tavern, Lufkin, Texas. He had his Jax and I had my Grapette.

"You ever hung a beer?" Pepper asked.

"No, sir," I replied.

"Why not?"

"I'm under age for one thing and Kansas State Highway Patrolmen do not drink alcoholic beverages."

"You're not a Kansas State Highway Patrolman."

"My dad is."

"Why not try a sip?"

"No, sir."

"You'd be a great Holy Road."

He asked the waitress for another glass. She was like Lillian the Come Lady only much, much fatter and younger and darker-haired and fully dressed in slacks and a blouse. I liked her because she didn't say a thing about my eyepatch and the hat. She was either a very nice person, or like the goofy guy at the Magnolia House, she thought she was stranger-looking than I was. Which wasn't true.

You would have thought Tom Bell Pepper Bowen was measuring out gold the way he divided up that bottle of beer into those two glasses. A tiny drop in one, then another in the other, a final two splashes and he was ready to turn me into a drunkard.

He lifted his glass. "To The One-Eyed Mack, the greatest pirate in Texas." He took a long sip and set his glass down on the table.

We were in a booth that had another one of those framed pictures of General Custer's Last Stand hanging on the wall right above it. Custer was standing there in the middle of his troops completely surrounded by Indians. One of his soldiers had already been scalped and an Indian with a knife between his teeth was pulling the hair back off the dead soldier's head. I wondered what genius figured that would get people to buy Budweiser beer.

"Do you hate that Indian scalping that guy there?" I asked Pepper.

"Nope."

"Do you hate Japs?"

"Nope."

"Who do you hate?"

"Pirates who won't try anything tough."

"Drinking beer ain't tough."

"Take a sip."

"No, sir," I said. "I told you I don't drink alcohol."

"Beer's not alcohol."

"Yeah it is."

"It's made out of wheat like you people grow in Kansas."

"Kansas wouldn't allow that. It's dry. You can't buy beer or anything else there and you have to go to Missouri for that. My dad catches bootleggers all the time and smashes up their stuff with sledgehammers at the courthouse like Carrie Nation did."

"Just see if it doesn't taste just like Kansas wheat."

Before I knew what I had done I had that glass up to my mouth and I had a mouthful. It was cold and musty and reminded me of iodine and castor oil and antifreeze and cold medicine and bus station restrooms. I put the glass down as fast as I could and worked at not spitting it up right there on the table in front of Pepper and General Custer and his dying soldiers.

"Now that wasn't bad, was it?" Pepper said, smiling as big as possible to smile.

"That is the worst-tasting stuff I have ever had in my mouth."

"It gets better, I promise. Try another sip. Make it smaller than the first."

I looked down at that awful glass of that awful stuff and decided, okay, one more little sip can't make it any worse than it already was.

I did it. It was about the same as the first. Then I had another and I realized that I was now on my way.

Whatever happened to the trooper's kid who called himself The One-Eyed Mack?

He drank himself to rack and ruin at the Lonesome Pine Tavern, Lufkin, Texas.

I drank the whole glass, which was really only half a bottle of beer. And I felt it. I don't mean I was drunk, really, but my head seemed a lighter weight than usual and way, way back in the deepest bottom of my throat I felt like there was the beginnings of a really good vomit. Nothing immediate or serious to worry about but it was there.

I decided not to go on toward Kansas tonight. It was already dark outside and, like Pepper said, there's always plenty of time to go home.

We asked a couple of people on the street and we looked around until we found the right place to spend the night. It was a big house that must have been somebody's mansion before it was turned into a rooming house. The sign out front was pretty old itself and said in white letters on a brown piece of wood, "Tourists." That was us. Him in his filthy white shirt and wrinkled striped blue suit and red tie and white straw hat and carrying his leather satchel. Me in my patch and hat and carrying the white sack from Roebaugh-Buck's.

The woman who ran the place was Mrs. Williams. She was at least the age of my grandmother, my momma's mother, so that made her at least sixty or seventy. Her hair was rotten-corn yellow and must have been a mile long because she had it wrapped and twisted and stacked almost a mile high on the top of her head. Her voice was soothing, like she had gone to expression class too long or played in a lot of Civil War movies.

The room she gave us was on the third floor in the very back. It was the cheapest, just three dollars for both of us. It had two narrow beds in the center of the room about two feet apart, a closet, and that was it except for a light in the ceiling. We put our stuff down and I said dibbies on the bathroom first and Pepper said fine. The bathroom was down the hall and I ran some bathwater and took a bath and it all made me feel great.

I could hardly wait for Tom Bell Pepper Bowen to do the same. His smell was really getting to me. But back in the room he made no move to go to the bathroom. He just lay there on his bed with those same clothes on, except he did take off his red tie and suit coat. I didn't say anything and just got into my bed.

"Are you really going on to Kansas tomorrow?" he asked after a while.

"Yeah. This kind of life isn't for me. I was born to spray blacktop and sickle weeds, I guess."

He didn't know what I was talking about, of course, so I told him about working for the county road department. His body smell was getting worse as each second went by. But he just kept lying there talking.

"We'd have been a good team, you and me," he said. "Pepper and The One-Eyed Mack."

"A team for doing what?"

"Pirating, preaching, bus ticketing, hanging Grapettes and Jax and telling lies. Things like that."

"How about quit telling lies to me?"

"Deal. Why do you say 'sir' to everybody?"

"That's the way I was taught."

I wanted to scream: "Go take a bath!" I knew I was going to gag and then vomit and then we'd have a real mess on our hands.

"What do you want to know the truth about?" he asked.

I didn't want to know anything right then until he got rid of his smell but I said, "Just any truth will do."

I heard him take a deep breath like he was about to talk for a very, very long time. "I was born in Alvarado, Texas, up between Cleburne and Dallas. My daddy was the son of a Holy Road preacher who believed God's worst punishment was giving him my daddy as his awful son...."

I sat straight up in the bed. "No! Shut up! Not one more word until you go down the hall to that bathroom and take a bath! Now! Go! Before I vomit! Go! Now!"

Pepper sprang straight up in his bed and stared right at me. Our noses weren't much more than about two feet apart. His face was dead serious when he said: "I can't take a bath."

"Water make you melt?"

"Not till I score."

"Score what?"

"In a burglary."

"You are crazy and you are a liar. Just a minute ago you promised not to lie...."

"Now you shut up, One-Eyed Mack! I am a burglar. You hear me. I am a burglar. That is the General Custer truth."

"You mean you crawl into people's bedrooms at night and steal their watches?"

"That's it."

"That's awful."

"I can't help it. That's what I was taught."

"Liar!"

"Believe what you want. But I am telling you we burglars have our superstitions and customs just like baseball players."

"Baseball players? Come on!"

"What do you know about baseball?"

"Everything."

"You ever heard of Smokey Slow Janecek of the Dodgers?"

"No, sir."

"Played shortstop in the late thirties and never bathed on days he didn't get a hit and not again until he did."

"What was the longest he went?"

"Once he had a thirty-four game batting slump."

"So you're saying you are not going to take a bath until you get a hit off somebody as a burglar?"

"That's what I'm saying, so you can either vomit or find yourself another room."

"You mean *you* find yourself another room, because it was my three dollars that paid for this room, please don't forget."

"Well, if you've got another five then I'll gladly get another room."

He said it straight, serious, like he was willing to do me that great favor by spending my money for him to move into another room.

Pepper and The One-Eyed Mack, otherwise known as Pepper and The One-Eyed Fool.

He lay back down and so did I. I decided that if I did throw up I would do it right on him. Nothing big or fancy and with no commotion. I'd just get up from my bed a second or two before it was coming and lean over his face and let him have it.

"To continue my family story, then," Pepper went on calmly. "I don't remember much about Alvarado...."

He had just confessed that he was a criminal element who was a burglar who would not take a bath until he committed another burglary. "... We moved from Alvarado shortly after I was born, out to Garden City in western Kansas, then to Cordell, Oklahoma; Pilot Point, Texas; Big Spring, Texas; Pryor, Oklahoma; Comanche, Texas; Nowata, Oklahoma; Iola, Kansas; Olpe, Kansas; Russell, Kansas; Del Rio, Texas; Hondo, Texas..."

I could not take it one more second. Not one more second.

"Get your satchel and let's go out and burglarize something," I said, grabbing a shirt and a pair of pants.

He was out of bed like a shot.

65

"You're a great person, One-Eyed Mack. A truly great person. If you had been with Custer I bet things would have turned out better."

"Yes, sir."

"Can I call you Mack for short?"

"No, sir."

Where did you go wrong, young man?

It started, Your Honor, when I met a stinky little Holy Road on the Texas Chief and lied to the conductor. Then I came in my pants on The Beaumont Rocket, plotted the breakup of a plumber's marriage and became a criminal.

Young man, do you have any advice for others on how to avoid the path of sin and crime your traveled?

Tell them never to go out and watch kids play kick-the-can.

We had trouble finding a place to burglarize. Tom Bell Pepper Bowen said there were rules. Never go inside a house at night unless you cased it in the daylight. Never hit a bank or a post office because they're federal and the FBI and J. Edgar Hoover will be after you with submachine guns. Never hit a tiny small business unless you know something about it because those people like to have dogs and traps and sirens and other crazy things hooked up to doors and windows. Pepper said one of his best friends and the best young burglar in north central Texas lost his left leg and his career at a typewriter repair shop in McKinney, Texas. There was a German shepherd dog inside who bit the leg completely off, and also had a bell tied to his neck and a rope to one leg; the rope went upstairs to the bedroom of the owner, who lived above the store. Pepper said his friend considered himself lucky that he got away alive.

We'd been out on the streets of Lufkin more than thirty minutes, looking for a good place that followed the rules, when I had one great idea.

"Let's hit the bus depot."

"They won't have anything in there except some lost suitcases and dirty urinals," Pepper said.

"There's something there I want and need," I said.

The bus depot was only three blocks from where we had that conversation. We came up to it from the rear through a parking lot where three buses were parked. Two of them were Texas Red Rocket Motor Bus Company Flxibles with the upside-down-comma scoop in the back. One of them looked just like the one we had come in on from the Beaumont.

The depot was completely dark. The only light inside was from the clocks on the wall, one that said "Bus Is Best" on the face, the other, "Always Going Your Way."

I wanted to make sure of only one thing before I went any further. "You really promise to take a bath when this is over?"

"General Custer honor."

"You promise?"

"Holy Road honor."

"Say you'll take a bath."

"I'll take a bath."

"Will you brush your teeth, too?"

"What's that got to do with this?"

"Your breath is bad."

"Okay."

"When is the last time you brushed your teeth?"

"I have false teeth."

"You're too young to have false teeth."

"I lost my real ones in a poker game in Fort Worth with the mayor, the governor of Texas and Enos Slaughter."

"I thought it was Ted Williams."

He took out what looked like a little coping-saw blade. He stuck it in the lock. The door opened.

It all happened before I could take another absolutely mortified, terrified breath.

I found what I wanted in less than a minute. It was the *Russell's Official National Motor Coach Guide,* a three-inch-thick book that came out every month with all the bus schedules in the country. Bus people called it the Red Guide because its cover was red. Molina, the night agent back home with Thunderbird, taught me how to read one.

The guide was right there on the ticket counter where I had seen it when we came in that afternoon. I picked it up and started looking at it and Pepper had a fit.

"Nobody breaks into a place to steal a book with bus schedules in it," he said. "Nobody."

"I'm not going to steal it. I'm just going to look up the schedules from here to Kansas, memorize them and leave the book here."

"It won't count as a real burglary then."

"Come on, you stinking little Bell Pepper!" I was hot.

So was he. "Burglars don't burglarize so one-eyed kid pirates can read a stupid bus book!"

"Well, I'm not stealing this guide and that's final!"

"Well, I'm not taking a bath and that's final!"

Young man, why did you take the Russell's Official National Motor Coach Guide?

I did it, Your Honor, so my new friend, Tom Bell Pepper Bowen, would take a bath.

I carried that guide back to the room like it was liquid TNT.

Pepper said it was all right with him if I dumped it in the first trashcan we came to, but I was afraid they would dust it for fingerprints and trace the crime right to me. Pepper said that was crazy because my prints weren't on file anywhere, but I knew more about any of that than he did because Dad was a Kansas State Highway Patrolman. Pepper kept saying he knew more than I did because he was a real burglar and I wasn't.

I put the guide under the mattress of my bed and stayed stark, wide-eyed awake like I was expecting a fist on the door any second.

This is the Texas Red Rocket Police! Come out with your hands up and the *Russell's Official National Motor Coach Guide* in them!

But I didn't mind not sleeping, to tell you the truth. Because when we got back to that room the first thing Pepper did was go down the hall to the bathroom. I heard the bathwater running and I heard him singing "Sweet Lorraine," and when he came back he smelled like Lava soap, the L-A-V-A kind that sponsored *Gangbusters* on the radio.

"Thanks, One-Eyed Mack," he said just before he fell asleep, like he was a baby and this was his nursery room or something.

"Thanks for what, exactly?"

"For helping me burglarize the bus depot."

"You're welcome, sir."

He turned over the other way and I got a particularly good

whiff of Lava soap. It was worth it even if the Texas Red Rocket Police did get me.

I could always plead insanity.

A tin can tore my left eye out, Your Honor, and turned me crazy.

I forgive you, One-Eyed Mack. God bless you and keep you.

6

Down the Holy Road

The first thing I noticed when I woke up the next morning was the smell of L-A-V-A soap from the next bed. Good. The second thing was that Pepper was not in that bed. Good.

Good, good, good!

So long, Tom Bell Pepper Bowen. You took me those first steps down the road of drink and crime. You forced Jax beer to my lips, a *Russell's Official National Motor Coach Guide* to my breast. But now I will put all of that behind me. Now I say good-bye to you and to your way of life. May you score often enough to keep yourself bathed. May you end up in clean prisons with nice guards.

May you never set foot in my town in Kansas, where seldom is heard a discouraging word and the deer and the antelope play.

But he hadn't gone anywhere except downstairs to wait for me. He was sitting in the parlor talking to a couple of Mrs. Williams's other tourists, a second-baseman type who said he had gone to college for three years to learn accounting and a centerfielder lumber-buyer from Louisiana.

"Time to pay a call on Jesus," said Pepper to me. "Care to join us at the Church of the Holy Road?" he said to the second baseman and the centerfielder.

Church? Was it Sunday?

"Yes, it is. Time to travel the Holy Road to Glory," Pepper said once we were outside. The other two declined the invitation.

"I'm traveling the road to Kansas now, thank you," I said. "Can't spare the time."

"A man who can't spare the time to travel the Holy Road for Jesus will fry like chicken batter in hell," he said.

I used to pretty much believe crazy stuff like that. I went to the Methodist Sunday school every week until Momma died. By the time Jimmy T. did my left eye in I was down to going maybe once a month or so. I knocked it off completely after that. God and Jesus and all their friends and preachers were supposed to look out after everyone who lived the right kind of life and did mostly the right kind of things. It didn't make sense then for Momma to die and my eye to get cut out. I know how all the talk goes. Dad tried it a little bit on me. So did Meg. But I said to both of them: Wait a minute. Momma was a wonderful person. Why kill her? Wait a minute. I was a really good kid. Did good in school, caused no trouble to anybody. There were eyes out there in kids a lot worse than me that could have been cut out with tin-can lids. Why mine?

I didn't even cuss!

But without really deciding to I was walking alongside Tom Bell Pepper Bowen down the Holy Road.

*　　*　　*

The church was small, frame and white, crowded and noisy. A man in a lemon sherbet–colored suit met us at the door with a handshake so strong, so energetic, so crushing I thought I was going to lose some fingers to Jesus as well as my soul.

He said we were on our way to Glory because we had come this morning to the Piney Woods Church of the Holy Road, Lufkin, Texas. He wanted our names and our hometowns and our home churches.

Pepper said he was Alton Flye James, his hometown was Nocona, Texas, and his home church was the First Church of the Holy Road, Van Alstyne, Texas. I gave my name as Roger Beaumont Lillian, my hometown was Mobile, Alabama, and my church was the Fifth Church of the Holy Road, Salina, Kansas.

I had come a long way since I told my first major adult lie to the conductor on the Texas Chief streamliner.

The man in the lemon-sherbet suit took his way down front to the third row on the aisle. He got some people to move over and scrunch up to make room for us. Visitors from faraway places, he told the scrunchers, who smiled at us like they really were glad to see us.

Before long, it started. We were on our feet singing a song I had never heard in the Methodist Church. It was all about blood on the cross and redemption and going to Glory. Everybody knew it by heart and sang it loudly like it was the Holy Road Star-Spangled Banner or something.

Everybody included Pepper. He really was a Holy Road. He also still smelled a bit of L-A-V-A, I was delighted to thank both the Methodist and the Holy Road Gods.

Then the preacher started talking. He was a quarterback kind of guy about forty, in cowboy boots and a dark green linen suit. He wasn't preaching really, but just telling stories about what it had been like working full-time on the Holy Road for Jesus the past week.

Suddenly a lady down front on the left was on her feet yelling about witnessing a devil spirit that came to visit her sick mother on Thursday. She asked for all of our prayers and everyone but me said, "Amen!"

She hadn't quite finished when a man right behind us was standing and crying out loud about a cousin who died in Springfield, Missouri. Then came another man confessing at the top of his lungs about how he did not stop to help a man with a flat tire the other night on the Jasper highway. A woman screamed out the story of how she lost her temper with her young son Darwin and hit him with a Jackson and Sons Hardware yardstick because he emptied a new bottle of Heinz catsup on the off-white shag rug in the living room.

With no warning, Tom Bell Pepper Bowen, alias Alton Flye James, was up on his feet beside me. Tears were running down his cheeks.

"Oh, brothers and sisters of the Holy Road, pray with me for my friend here. Pray, pray, pray!" His left hand was on my shoulder. He was talking about me.

"Within the last day he has sinned. Oh, how he has sinned. He has taken something that belonged to another. Something that was not his to take. Something that he took in the dead of night.

"Pray for him, brothers and sisters of the Holy Road. Pray that he will cleanse his soul of this sin by confessing it now to us all so he may go on down the Holy Road to Glory."

Every one of those crazy Holy Roads in that place was now staring right at me. And yelling at me.

"Confess!" "Do it, Brother!" "Confess!" "Take the Holy

74

Road!" "Confess!" "Cleanse yourself, Brother!" "Confess!" "Confess!" "Confess!"

The preacher came down off his pulpit to me. He got down on one knee there in the aisle, put his right hand on my left shoulder, closed his eyes tight and bowed his head. In a play-by-play radio-announcer voice he yelled: "Oh, Jesus, please, please help this young man, this sinning child of God. Help him hear the voice that will stand him on his feet, and say the words that will set him free from his sin and show him the way down the Holy Road to Glory."

I had two revelation kinds of things at that moment. Thing One was that there was no way these lunatics were ever letting me out of here until I stood up and yelled out something. Thing Two was that if I survived this experience I was going to make it my life's work to pay back Tom Bell Pepper Bowen, alias Alton Flye James, for what he did to me.

Thing One was first.

I stood up and everybody, including the preacher, shut up.

"I confess here in front of all of you and Jesus in Heaven that last night while everyone slept I stole something that did not belong to me. I stole it because I am no good."

I took a breath and the people of the Piney Woods Church of the Holy Road yelled, "Amen!" "Glory!"

"I am rotten to the core. I am full of sin. I am wicked. I am worthless...."

"Amen!" "Glory!"

"It happened because I wear this evil eyepatch ..."

"Amen!"

"... And I carry this Roebaugh-Buck's bag ..."

"Amen!"

"... and wear this funny hat ..."

"Amen!"

75

There was a rhythm going now. And it was fun.

"I also lied to the conductor on the Texas Chief streamliner . . ."

"Amen!"

". . . and planned the breakup of the marriage of one of God's chosen plumbers. . . ."

"Amen!"

I decided to skip Lillian the Come Lady and The Beaumont Rocket.

"And I failed to pattern my life after this devoted man of the Holy Road, Alton Flye James of the First Church of the Holy Road, Van Alstyne, Texas."

"Amen!"

They loved me. And they didn't even seem to notice that I never said exactly what it was I stole last night and where I stole it.

We sang another song I didn't know, the preacher preached a sermon on how love can be divided and spread around like Jesus did the fishes and the loaves of bread. The collection plates were passed among us. Pepper insisted in a whisper that I put in a dollar bill, four bits for each of us. I noticed the L-A-V-A smell was wearing off.

The invitation was next and last. And it was embarrassing and awful. We were on the third verse of the third invitational hymn and nobody had yet come down front to give themselves to Jesus.

We sang the fourth verse. Still nobody came.

"Won't you come! Won't you come?" said the preacher. Sweat was showing through the arms of the dark green suit.

"Take that walk, Brother. Take that walk down that aisle to Glory," he said. "Jesus is the Way and Here is the Way to Jesus."

"Won't you come? Won't you come?"

He said it a thousand times. A million times. Still nobody came.

Won't you come?

Why not call it off, Mister Preacher? Why not chalk it up as a bad day at the office and forget it until next Sunday?

It was then that stupid me realized Tom Bell Pepper Bowen and just about every other Holy Road in that church were looking at me. Me. I was being invited specially to take a walk down that aisle to Glory.

Well, they could sing all four verses of 103 hymns through 103 times and The One-Eyed Mack, retired pirate on his way back to Kansas, was not going to budge. That was final.

"This will never end until you go up there," Pepper whispered in my ear when we were about to third verse, seventh song.

"No way," I spit back. I mean I spit, too. Some got on his nose, which was what he deserved.

"They need one good convert this morning."

"You go."

"I'm already saved."

"From what?"

"Sin."

"You're a burglar."

"So are you now."

We moved to the next song, first verse. The voices were sounding hoarser and hoarser. The preacher's "won't you comes" were getting more and more pleading. Like his life depended on it.

"Go up there or this will never, ever end, I am telling you," Pepper said. "You're all he's got in his sights this morning. Go or we all stay."

"For how long?"

"I was at one once where it went on for fourteen hours before somebody answered the invitation."

"What do I have to do?" I asked. In fourteen hours I planned to be back in my own bed in Kansas.

"Go up there, kneel and cry while he prays for you."

"I can't just cry like that."

"Think of something awful."

"Like what?"

"Like what happened to your left eye."

"I hate you."

"God forgives you because you know not what you say."

The place went nuts when I got up and started down that aisle. I mean wild. They hooted and hollered and clapped and prayed and screamed "Amen!" and "Glory!" like Jesus Himself had just walked in off the street.

I had never felt so powerful in my life.

There was a rah-rah catcher of a kid named Randy Martin Salisbury who came to our town and Carrie Nation High in the middle of the tenth grade from Garden City. His father was a transformer mechanic for Kansas Power and Light. The very first minute of the very first day he came to school Randy and I became best friends. The first minute. I saw that he had a St. Louis Cardinals sticker on his loose-leaf notebook and I asked him what Stan the Man's batting average was the year he broke in.

Randy, without so much as changing the scared look he had on his face, said: "It was forty-one. He played in twelve games and hit .426. How about his first full season?"

"He hit .315," I said quickly. "Where was he born?"

"Donora, Pennsylvania. When?"

"November 21, 1920. How many homers did he hit last year?"

"Thirty-six."

From then on we ate every lunch together, played ball and swam together, went to the bathroom together, watched and talked girls together, studied together and palled around everywhere together. We did it that way until the minute he left for Winfield, where Kansas Power and Light sent his dad next. That was in the first couple of months of the twelfth grade and I haven't seen or heard a word from or about him since. But he was the closest friend I had in the world for those nearly two years and as close as any friend I've ever had. There are people I have known all my life that I wouldn't call to help me take out a splinter from my big toe. But after only two days of knowing each other I could have asked Randy to give me either one of his big toes and he would have given it to me and I would have done the same for him.

I have always known for sure that losing the left eye would have gone a lot better if Randy had been around.

I don't know what it is that makes some people really hit it off the way Randy and I did but I felt it was there again between Pepper and me. At least it looked like it was finally heading that way. You never know.

It's crazy how things happen. What if Randy hadn't known what Stan the Man did his rookie year? What if I hadn't known Stan's birthday?

What if I hadn't been on that Texas Chief streamliner that day? What if I hadn't decided to take the bus to Lufkin, too?

But I was still sure I was going back home. Fairly sure.

We were walking back to town. As soon as we were out

of eye and shot of the church I gave Pepper a shove into the street. He laughed and laughed.

A car was coming. "Run him over!" I yelled at the car, which had no trouble missing him. "He deserves to die."

Pepper was bent over laughing. " 'I am rotten to the core because I carry this white bag. I sinned because I wear this evil eyepatch. . . .' "

"You are the worst person God ever created," I said. And laughed. I couldn't help it.

"You are the best Holy Road confessor I have ever seen," he said.

I pushed him into the street again. But not very hard.

We arrived at the courthouse square. There was a bench at one corner in front of the big courthouse building in front of a statue. Why not sit down and take a break before you are on your way to Kansas? he asked. Why not?

The statue was of a World War One soldier in full battle dress. He had a rifle in one hand and a grenade in the other. His mouth was open and he seemed to be yelling something at the Germans. There was an honor roll of names of the men from Lufkin who had died in the war on the pedestal below. Capt. C. M. McConnell, Lloyd Kelly Grapp, Miles T. H. Parris, Clarence E. Murray, Phillip W. Schmidt, Joe Paul Satter, Curtis T. Sealey, C. Dover Shofner, Weaver Plez Cox, Burt C. Battendorf and others. I counted thirty-five names.

I wondered what they had been doing there in Lufkin before they went to war? How did you die, Burt C. Battendorf? Who did you leave behind? Do they still cry at night because you're not there? Did God decide you should be one of the thirty-five? Or did somebody pull names out of a hat? Were you a Holy Road?

Why wasn't there a statue here for the World War Two

guys? How many from Lufkin died in that one? What are their names?

Then from way down the street I saw my dad coming. The best state trooper in Kansas had tracked his son to a bench in front of a statue of a dead World War One soldier in Lufkin, Texas. He was still four or five blocks away but I was sure it was him because of the walk. He walked like Alan Ladd did in the movies and unless it was Alan Ladd it just had to be my dad.

There couldn't be three people in America who walked like Alan Ladd.

He had probably picked up my trail from the Texas Chief conductor. The Mexican kid at the cafeteria and the Texas Red Rocket Motor Bus Company ticket agents and drivers told all. So did the plumber and the guy at the newspaper office. Lillian. Please, Lord of the Holy Road, let it be that he did not know what Lillian and his only son did on The Beaumont Rocket. And that he didn't know about the *Russell's Official National Motor Coach Guide.* Or that I had just agreed in front of a bunch of screaming ninnies to follow the Holy Road to Glory.

My first idea was to run. But that was crazy. He was my dad, after all, and he had spent a lot of money and time finding me and it would hardly be fair to foul it all up now and cost him even more money. Besides, I was on my way home to Kansas anyhow.

Almost. More or less.

I didn't tell Pepper until it was too late for him to run away. His face turned a little like a prune but there was nothing there like the terror when the conductor came down the aisle of our car on the Texas Chief streamliner. I wanted him to meet Dad before we split and went off like my other close friend Randy Martin Salisbury and me and never saw each other again.

But it wasn't Dad. There were three men in America who walked like Alan Ladd.

At a half-block away I saw this third one was also two inches shorter and fifty pounds lighter than Dad and he walked with his head looking down, like a pitcher who had just been knocked out of the box after giving up five runs in the last of the eighth. Dad always walked with his chin up and back.

"You figure your dad's looking for you?" Pepper asked with great relief when I told him it wasn't Trooper Dad after all.

"I'm sure he is."

"Why?"

"Because he loves me and he's worried about me. I should have called him from Galveston and told him I was going to be a pirate."

"What would he have said?"

"I don't know. Did you call your dad and tell him you were going to be a burglar?"

"He already knew."

"How?"

The third man in America who walked like Alan Ladd had gone on by us but at the corner he turned around and was now standing right in front of the bench and us. I had never seen a man as tired as he looked like he was. His eyes and his eyebrows and his ears and even the hairs in his nose drooped like there were lead sinkers on them. He was in his late thirties maybe, about Dad's age, but somewhere else in him he was as old as Grandfather Moore, Momma's dad. He wasn't a bum or anything. He was shaved and his gray suit and black tie and white shirt were fairly clean.

He looked at us, but at our feet not our faces.

"Would either of you gentlemen be interested in buying a Humble Oil map of Texas?"

His voice was crisp, like a man from Macomb, Illinois, who came through town once selling lawnmowers and rubber garden hoses that nobody seemed to need or want to buy.

"No thank you," said Pepper.

"How much?" I said.

"One dollar."

He took the map out of a coat pocket. The map was torn and old.

"I'll take it," I said, and pulled out a dollar bill.

He took it and gave me the map. "It's not the whole state, to be perfectly honest about it," he said, still talking only to my shoes. "The top Panhandle part from Amarillo to Dalhart is missing. I tore it off so I wouldn't ever forget the map. It was made by the Gosha Map Company."

"Thank you, sir."

"I'm going to Austin to see the governor of Texas," he said, and walked away. Pepper was beside himself.

"You do know they give away brand-spanking-new road maps at every filling station in the world?"

"Yes, sir."

"Then why did you just do that?"

"He needed a dollar."

"Real pirates do not give away their own money, One-Eyed Mack," he said, like he was giving a lecture on the radio. "Real pirates give away other people's money."

"I'm not a real pirate."

He took the map from me and unfolded it across our laps.

"Let's go to Houston," he said after a minute or two of hard study.

"Where is it exactly?"

"There." He pointed to a large round dot down at the bottom. It was just above a smaller dot of Galveston.

"That's not toward Kansas. Isn't that back down the way we came?"

"Who knows? Who cares?"

He grabbed his satchel. I folded up the old map and picked up my white Roebaugh-Buck's bag.

We walked off together toward the bus station.

7
A Different Kind of Pirate

We came up the back way through the parking lot again where the buses were kept. It was the same way we had traveled only hours before as burglars. It was spooky. Only one of the Texas Red Rocket Motor Bus Company Flxibles was there and it looked sad, lonely and forgotten. It reminded me of how awful it was to eat a tunafish-salad sandwich and a Grapette in a restaurant all by myself and I wondered if having that upside-down-comma scoop coming out of its rear was for a bus what not having a left eye was for humans.

Before I knew what I'd done I had the door open to it and was climbing up inside.

"What are you doing?" Pepper asked, following me into the bus.

"Just looking around," I said.

"You want to take it to Houston?"

"What do you mean *take* it?"

"I mean pirate it."

"What do you mean pirate it?"

"You and I close this bus's door, turn on its motor and drive it to Houston and maybe around the world. That's what pirating is."

"That's stealing."

"Wait here," he said. "I'll be right back."

I waited there inside that bus all right and in a few minutes Pepper was back with two teenage colored girls, an old white man with a cane and a whole Mexican family of father, mother and four children of all kinds of ages. He helped them on the bus like he was an official Texas Red Rocket Motor Bus Company driver. He sat down in the driver's seat behind the steering wheel and closed the door.

"All aboard for Houston!" he yelled.

"You ever driven a bus like this before?" I asked as I moved up to the first passenger seat right behind him. "Who are these people?"

"They were just hanging around waiting to go to Houston. I whispered that if they came with me and didn't say anything to anybody then I would take them to Houston free of charge. Just like a good pirate would." In a few seconds he had the motor going. "No, I haven't driven a bus like this before. Have you?"

"No, sir."

"It's just like a car only wider and longer and slower."

There were some loud scrapes as he got that poor Flxible's gears into first.

We lurched off. He turned the steering wheel like he almost knew what he was doing and there we were out of the parking lot and onto the street.

"On to Houston!" Pepper hollered into the rearview mirror at me and the other passengers.

I yelled: "Houston, Houston, here we come! Houston, Houston here we come!"

That did it for the two teenage girls. They were on their feet in the middle of the aisle. "Stop this bus! Stop this bus!" one of them screamed. "We want off of here!" screamed the other.

It took Pepper a while to bring the bus eventually to a dead stop at the curb. He opened the bus door and those two girls hopped off like somebody was holding a welding torch to their behinds.

"You people are crazy," they said almost in unison as they departed our lives.

True.

I hadn't noticed until right then that we just happened to stop in front of Mrs. Williams's rooming house. Before Pepper could get the door closed and the bus going again Mrs. Williams was out her front door hustling down the sidewalk toward us.

"Bus driver," she said. "Mister bus driver. Hold that bus. I have a passenger. . . ."

She saw Pepper behind the wheel. Then she saw me. She smiled and climbed up into the stairwell of the bus. Her hair was still rotten-corn yellow and stacked high on her head.

"I didn't realize you two gentlemen were in transportation," she said. "This isn't a regular schedule, is it? Where are you going?"

"To Houston, ma'am," I said. "It's a free bus. The Holy Road church hired us to take people down any road they want to go down."

"I have a passenger for you."

She almost flew up to her house and in a flash was on her

way back our way with the Map Man, the third man in America who walked like Alan Ladd.

"Here we are now," she said to him, helping him on the bus. "These nice men will take you where you want to go."

"We're going to Houston, ma'am," I said.

"I'm going to Austin to see the governor of Texas," the Map Man said.

"Yes, but this bus isn't going to Austin."

"I'm sure you boys will work out something." Mrs. Williams scooted down out of that bus and was gone up the sidewalk moving almost as fast as those teenage girls did.

The Map Man sat down next to me right behind Pepper. "Do you need a map?" he asked.

"No, sir."

"I have one of Nebraska. It's a Skelly Oil. Seventy-five cents is the price."

"I'll take it," I said.

I gave him a half-dollar and a quarter and he handed me the Skelly Oil map of Nebraska. It was old and yellow and cracked just like the one of Texas.

"To be honest about it," said the Map Man, "part of it from Omaha down to Falls City is missing. I tore it off so I wouldn't forget it. It's a Rand McNally."

"That's fine, sir."

He got up and moved to a seat by himself halfway back in the bus.

The old Humble Oil map of Texas said U.S. Highway 59 was the way to Houston. After a couple of wrong turns and slow reads and shouted questions out the window, we were on it and really on our way. It was only then I came to hard grips with what was going on here.

We were bus thieves. The Texas Red Rocket Motor Bus people, whoever they were, were short a little Flxible bus right about now because we stole it and we were driving it to Houston with an old man, a Mexican family and the third man in the world who walks like Alan Ladd and who sells old road maps with parts torn off, never looks anyone in the eye and thinks he's on his way to see the governor of Texas in Austin. If they hang cattle thieves on courthouse squares in Texas, what would be the punishment for bus thieves?

I wondered if anybody had ever stolen a bus before in Texas or anywhere else? I leaned up and asked Pepper that.

"No, Mister One-Eyed Mack," he said, "we're charting new ground here. We are the first bus pirates in the history of the United States of America. That grandson of yours will be proud to hear you discussed in American history classes."

Grandson?

" 'Hey there, One-Eyed Mack the Third, tell the class all about your grandfather, our country's first bus pirate,' " is what the teacher will say."

Our country's first bus pirate.

Where did he go wrong, Mister Trooper Dad?

It started on the Texas Chief streamliner, Your Honor. That's all we know.

Had he ever shown signs that he might steal a Flxible bus, Mister Trooper Dad?

No, Your Honor. He was always mostly just a St. Louis Cardinals fan.

We pulled into a drive-in restaurant there on the highway in the middle of a town. It was beginning to get dark and we were hungry.

Pepper blew the bus horn as loud as he could. A cheerleader-type girl in a yellow and blue cheerleader-type outfit came prancing out as fast as her perfectly formed legs would carry her. She came around to the driver's window where Pepper was and giggled and said she wasn't used to waiting on buses, only cars, pickup trucks and Cushman motor scooters. Cushman motor scooters.

Cushman motor scooters were what my major dream Number Two was about. Right after the Trooper Dream I loved most to close my eyes and see myself on a red Cushman with a cheerleader-type girl sitting on the seat behind me holding on around my stomach for dear life.

The old man with the cane said he wanted an order of french fries. The Mexican family was named Santos. None of them spoke much English, but each said Dr Pepper one at a time. It took me a stupid minute or two to figure out they meant that prune-juice soda pop they had in Texas, instead of something to do with Tom Bell Pepper Bowen. The Map Man said he was trying to trim down before he saw the governor of Texas, so all he wanted was a root beer float. I ordered my regular tuna sandwich and a Grapette and Pepper got a cheeseburger with lettuce, tomato and mayonnaise plus a Dr Pepper. I couldn't imagine anything worse than eating a cheeseburger with mayonnaise and washing it down with a soda pop that was carbonated prune juice.

I was sure Pepper the Crook was tempted to drive the bus off without paying the cheerleader, but I wasn't going to let him so that was that and he knew it. I paid the $3.25 and Pepper got off to find a restroom.

I decided to check on our passengers. The crazy map man. I asked him where he lived. Joplin, Missouri, he said. What was he doing in Texas? Business. Where did he get those fine old maps? Joplin, Missouri. How many others did he have? Too many to count. What did he do with them? Studied them and folded them mostly. He reminded me of the short-order cook in Beaumont who didn't talk. Did the Japs force U.S. prisoners to collect oil company road maps as punishment, too?

I went over to see the man with the cane. He was old, maybe fifty or fifty-five, but seemed completely sane and with it most of the time. He smiled and held on for dear life to his cane, which was shiny-white like a broom handle, like it really was keeping him alive somehow. He said he had a daughter in Houston who loved him more than she did her mother, who was now dead, and she would be waiting for him at the bus station in Houston. He said he retired as a fireman two years ago after he fell off a ladder truck on the way to a fire in Lufkin and cracked his skull and broke his left leg in eight places. He said he sure did thank us for taking him to Houston on this free Holy Road bus.

I just smiled at the Santos family.

We had just hit the outskirts of the next town when out of nowhere came the worst thunderstorm I had ever seen in my life. Hail as big and as hard as those balls the Cardinals used pounded the top of our little bus like we were the enemy in some war. The wind blew so hard the rain came down sideways across the road and it was all but impossible to see much of anything in front of us.

Pepper pulled off into a Shell station. It had a covered front and the bus fit nicely under it. The station was closed and there was nobody around but I had a sudden thought that if the Map Man knew Pepper was a burglar he would want him to break into the place and steal some maps. Maybe they have a great one of Oklahoma. He hasn't said anything about

Oklahoma. I wondered what part of Oklahoma he would tear off? How about an Arkansas?

The sound of the hail and the thunder and the rain on the metal roof above us was awesome. The lightning, when it came just before the thunder, lit up the dark station and everything around it like some drunk was playing with one of those movie searchlights. I heard the Santos kids in back talking like crazy in Spanish. They were scared. So was I. I couldn't tell about Pepper. He just sat there in the driver's seat half turned toward the side and me. We were talking about families.

"Where's your dad now?" I asked.

"Up north."

"Doing what?"

"Resting."

"Where's your mother?"

"West Virginia. She's resting, too."

A clap of thunder crashed and I swear I felt our little Flxible sway. We had thunderstorms in Kansas but never as bad as this thing was. I began to wonder if we were going to get out of this one alive. Seriously.

But Pepper just ignored it, like we were having a chat at a Rexall. Our baseball coach at Carrie Nation was like that. The score could be 1 to 1 in the last of the ninth with the bases loaded and a full count at the plate and Coach Katt never changed his expression or raised his voice or sweat a pearl. He dropped dead from a heart attack the next year after I graduated and nobody could figure out why. He was only forty-two and had never been sick a day in his life. He had played minor-league ball for a Phillies farm club in Missouri and they sent a scout to the funeral. Several of my buddies were hoping he might spot one of us in the church during the funeral and offer a big-league contract. I told them that never in the history of baseball had anybody ever been signed from just being seen at a funeral, but they didn't listen.

Nobody listened to me much after I lost my eye. Not even Dad and Meg, to be fully honest about it. Maybe they could tell even then that I was going to turn bad on the Texas Chief streamliner and become one of this country's first two bus pirates.

"You have any brothers or sisters?" I asked Pepper.

"An older brother named Jake is all. He writes obituaries for a newspaper in Anniston, Alabama."

"So that's where that business came from."

"Everything comes from something."

"Thank you, sir."

Then somebody came up to the bus door and banged on the window with a fist. Pepper opened it quickly and a young guy stepped inside. He looked like one of those scums with greasy hair and pimples and tattoos we all knew in school who couldn't read out loud in the seventh grade, smoked cigarettes in the eighth, hit a teacher in the ninth, and were gone forever in the tenth.

He looked at Pepper and at me and our passengers in the back, sighed with what to me seemed like disappointment and pulled a Louisville Slugger baseball bat out from behind his back.

"I want your money, your watches and everything else," he said in a Texas-y voice that was phony tough. "Make it swift or I start using some heads for baseballs."

"What model bat is that?" I asked.

"It's a Gil Hodges," said the Scum.

"The best first baseman in the National League right now. Size?"

"Thirty-six inches."

I told him we were poor people and we didn't have watches and money and things like that. Pepper told him that besides we were thieves, too, and thieves didn't go around stealing from one another. It was unethical and would give the business a bad name. The Scum, he was twenty-four maybe but he seemed older, didn't think that was very funny and he stepped up to Pepper and put the fat top part of the bat right up under his chin.

"I'm counting to ten and then it's all over for you, little man," he said.

Then he turned toward me and said, "Give me that hat of yours."

"No way," I said.

He started to raise the bat like he was going to swing it at my head, when like the lightning outside, Tom Bell Pepper Bowen barreled into the Scum's stomach headfirst. The guy fell back down the two steps to the ground outside. Pepper and I jumped on him. The old man with the cane was right behind us and he hit the kid in the head with his cane eight or nine times until I asked him to stop. The Santos father and the three largest of his four kids were there like a flash and they each took a hand or a finger or a foot to stand or sit on. The last man to the rescue was the Map Man but he did have the thirty-six-inch Gil Hodges Louisville Slugger in his hand. The Scum had dropped it when Pepper hit him.

After a few seconds of conversation we decided we would teach this young man a lesson that crime does not pay if it is directed at Pepper and The One-Eyed Mack, America's first bus pirates, and friends. I argued in favor of holding him by his heels outside a window all the way to Houston or trying to stuff him headfirst into the upside-down-comma air-scoop up on top. Pepper said both were bad ideas because they would attract the attention of passing police cars and other people. Besides, he said, and I agreed, who wants to take this scum around the world with us?

So Pepper took the long, thin burglary tool from his valise and opened the front door to the Shell station as the Scum pleaded for his life and limb and promised to never again try to rob us. He said he was walking home from the Baptist church and had taken cover from the storm under a big tree across the street. He saw our bus and us sitting there and the urge to rob us just came to him. It was the first time he had ever thought of doing anything like that and the idea must have come from the evil spirit in the lightning and thunder.

"I've heard of it raining violets and puppy dogs and a lot of other strange things but I don't think I've ever heard of a case of it raining Louisville Sluggers," said Pepper. "Have you, One-Eyed Mack?"

"No, sir. Particularly Gil Hodges models."

"I take my bat with me everywhere," said the Scum. "You never know when somebody's going to work up a game."

In April? In a storm?

With the help of all our passengers we got the guy inside the little filling-station office. We stuck the Louisville Slugger down the front of his pants so the fat, heavy end came at about the crotch and the narrow handle end up around his left ear. Then we wrapped and tied some electric wires around him in a way that held the bat tight and secure up his middle and his hands and arms tight and secure along each side.

Then Pepper and I had a real argument over what to do with the Scum's money. We found fifty-five dollars in cash in his pants pocket and Pepper said we should take it.

"That makes us just like him," I said. "I don't want to be

like him and you don't want to be like him, and the Map Man and the man with the cane and the Santos family don't want to be like him."

"What do we do with it, then? He stole it from people and to let him keep it would be unethical."

"Got it," I said in a flash. I took the money and opened the cash register up by the front window, stuck the money in the empty drawer and closed it. "Now the guy who runs this place will have a little special present when he opens up in the morning."

Tom Bell Pepper Bowen loved that idea and shook my hand like I was Stan the Man. "Your grandson will be proud to tell this story," he said. "You are the very best."

I felt he was probably right.

"You are free to go, Scum," I said to the Scum. "Go."

"Like this?" he said, looking down at the Louisville Slugger growing upward out of his pants.

"Like that."

He waddled out the door and back into the rain, which had lightened up considerably.

My eye caught a small metal rack behind the cash register that was stuffed with Shell road maps. I suggested to the Map Man that he go over and help himself.

He looked at my shoes in horror. "I only collect the old ones," he said.

Pepper insisted I drive the bus. I told him that wouldn't be smart or safe because I had only one eye, the roads were wet, it was dark and I had driven a car only twice before in my life, and both times were with my Uncle Marvin in Independence, whose car was an old Buick that wouldn't go more than twenty-five miles an hour. The only car we ever had was Dad's state highway patrol car and I couldn't drive that. But Pepper said I just had to drive the bus. How could it be a real pirate bus if the real pirate never drove it?

It took me a few minutes to get the hang of changing gears and double clutching but he showed me how and I practiced there in front of the service station before I drove it out on the highway.

I felt like Glory had come. This was it. Sitting up there behind that wheel, shifting those gears, applying those hissing air brakes, blowing the air horn, dimming the headlights, looking back at my passengers in the rearview mirror.

For the first time I felt like I really was the real One-Eyed Mack.

Pepper said, "Let's sing."

"Hey, hey, let's sing," I said.

> "Bringing in the sheaves,
> Bringing in the sheaves,
> We shall come rejoicing
> Bringing in the sheaves. . . ."

Pepper started and I was with him by the second "Bringing." So, surprisingly, was the Map Man, even though he looked down and at the dark out the window as he sang, in a fabulous voice that reminded me a lot of the choir director's at our Methodist church. The man with the cane didn't seem to know all the words but he hummed along loudly when he came to one he couldn't remember. Even the Santos family sang along in Spanish.

Whatever happened to the trooper's kid who lost the eye in a kick-the-can game?

He became the country's first bus pirate and he sang "Bringing in the Sheaves" while driving a stolen Texas Red Rocket Motor Bus Company Flxible down U.S. Highway 59 to Houston.

8

Trooper Dad

I could see the lights of Houston long before we actually got there. It was a very huge place. I wanted Pepper to take over but he said, "Take it on in," like he was General Dwight David Eisenhower on D Day.

I took it on in, to and through at least fifty stops and starts at stop signs and lights by the time I finally halted the bus in front of a bar-café on a side street three blocks from the Continental Trailways bus depot downtown. Some of those stops were also to ask directions of people who must have wondered why a one-eyed guy was driving a bus and why he didn't know where the bus station was. I would have loved to have driven our little Texas Red Rocket right up to the bus depot loading dock but Pepper and I decided that would not be the smartest thing for America's first two bus pirates in a stolen bus.

It was ten minutes before ten o'clock, said the Pearl Beer clock in the café window.

We walked the man with the cane and the Santos family

over to the bus depot and said so long. I gave the family a five-dollar bill to help on their trip on to Corpus Christi. They hugged us both and called Pepper Dr. Pepper.

But the Map Man would not go away. He would not get off our little bus.

"You told me you would take me to Austin to see the governor," he said firmly to the floor of the Flxible.

I told him I would pay for him to ride a regular scheduled bus and it would be the same.

"You told me you would take me to Austin to see the governor," he said again to the floor.

Pepper told him the regular bus would be bigger and faster and would probably get him to Austin sooner than we could with our little bus and our little experience as bus drivers.

"You told me you would take me to Austin to . . ."

"How far is Austin?" I asked Pepper.

"Two hundred fifty miles. Something like that."

"How about it, then?"

"Hey, come on, Mister Pirate, we've got pirating to do. Maybe drive on back to Galveston and do it right for you. . . ."

"On to Austin," I said.

"Okay, on to Austin," he said with a head shake that let me know he thought the whole thing was crazy. True, but so what?

"You drive," I said.

I got out of the driver's seat and he slipped in. He closed the Flxible's door and pushed the starter button. Nothing happened. Not a whir, not a click, not a sound. Then he looked at the dashboard carefully and turned around to me with the kind of smile Coach Katt gave me every time I booted a grounder at second base.

"You left the headlights on, Mister One-Eyed Mack. The battery's dead. Stone dead."

I took a ten-dollar bill, folded it up and stuck it in the crack around the horn button in the center of the steering wheel. I told Pepper that was for the gas we used and for getting the battery recharged. Pepper said the Texas Red Rocket Bus people should pay us for what we did, because of the honor we brought to their Flxible as the first bus ever used by the first bus pirates in the history of America. Rah, rah.

Then he did the most wonderful thing. He reached into his satchel case and pulled out that awful dirty white shirt he had worn the first few days I knew him. It was all wadded up and it stunk to high heaven. He carefully wiped the steering wheel, the various buttons on the dashboard, the door handle and just about every other metal or hard thing there was in the front of the bus. He did it quickly, like he knew what he was doing because he had done it a time or two before.

"Worried about your fingerprints?" I said.

"No, not mine," he said, wiping some light switches on the left. "Yours."

"Mine?"

"They already know all about me. No point in getting you messed up, too."

The only problem was that every place he wiped was then coated with his terrible smell. Talk about leaving a trail! I thought it was good they didn't keep b.o. prints on file at the FBI, like fingerprints, or we wouldn't stand a chance.

Pepper grabbed his satchel and I took my white Roebaugh-Buck's bag and we and the Map Man stepped down and off of our little Flxible. Pepper shut the door so any prints on it would be his. It was dark but there were street lights around, so I could see the little bus and its upside-down-comma air-scoop one last, long time.

I wanted to hug it like it was a person or a dog or a horse—something alive.

"We should have given her a name," I said to Pepper.

"Who says buses are hers?"

"Look at her and tell me she isn't a her."

Pepper puckered up his nose and his eyes like he was a doctor looking at somebody's sore throat. "Okay, she's a her," he said. "What name did you have in mind?"

"I don't have one. . . ."

"Gertrude!" yelled the Map Man in that same loud and sure voice he had used to sing "Bringing in the Sheaves." I may have been mistaken but it also seemed to me like he actually looked at Pepper and me for a second. A quick second.

"Who is Gertrude?" asked Pepper.

"The woman I love," the Map Man said to the ground. "She's the reason I have to go to Austin to see the governor."

"Then Gertrude she is!" yelled Pepper.

"Three cheers for Gertrude!" I yelled.

"Let's go hang a Jax or two and christen her right," Pepper said, and we marched into the Buffalo Bayou Tap Room, which was right there by us.

It was the third bar I had been into in two days, the third in my life. It was almost identical to that first two in Beaumont and Lufkin. There wasn't much light or many customers, the jukebox played hillbilly music too loud, the bartender was an old man who didn't smile, the waitresses looked like Lillian the Come Lady, and the decorations behind the bar were lit-up ads for Jax, Pearl, Lone Star and other beer companies. This one, also like the other two, had that same colored Budweiser painting of General Custer's Last Fight on the wall. Was there a law in Texas requiring every bar to have one?

I went over and looked again at the thing, which was a yard wide and a good two feet high. There must have been 200 soldiers and Indians shooting, stabbing, grabbing and scalping one another. Custer there in the center was dressed in a tan Kit Carson–Buffalo Bill kind of frontiersman's leather outfit. He had long hair and a big mustache and a red bandana flying out from around his neck. He was waving a sword in his right hand, a pistol in his left. But he had hold of the pistol's barrel like it was out of ammunition and all he could hope to do now was bash the Indians with its butt.

Clearly, General Custer was only a few minutes away from traveling down the final leg of the Holy Road to his final Glory.

Pepper immediately ordered three Jax beers when we sat down. The Map Man told the table he hadn't allowed alcohol of any kind to touch his lips or contaminate his mouth, throat and stomach since he left Gertrude, but this was such a special occasion it would be sinful and disrespectful not to join in the celebration of naming that bus after the woman he loved.

I hated everything about the taste, but before I knew what I had done I drank Beer One as quickly as Pepper and the Map Man did theirs.

Why not let's have another? said Pepper. Why not? The taste got better on Beer Two and it went down easier and I began to feel really great. Everything everybody said, particularly everything I said, was big and clever and smart and I never laughed so much in my life. The Map Man, who also had a second one, even laughed and cut up with us a bit although I didn't see him look at anything other than the table most of the time.

One more for the road? I couldn't believe Pepper suggested it and I couldn't believe I said that was one great idea.

I got only the first sip of Beer Three down the throat when things started happening to me that had never happened before. I was sitting there listening to Pepper and the Map Man talking about the best way to shift a stick shift into reverse on a Ford pickup. Pepper said you should crush it right up to the left from neutral and the Map Man said, no, that would strip those gears right out of there so the best way was to rest it in neutral for a count of three before nudging it ever so slowly up there. I couldn't tell if either one of them knew or cared a lick about it and I knew I certainly didn't.

Then suddenly my eyes went funny and there were at least two Peppers and a half dozen Map Mans. My face got hot like I had diphtheria or chicken pox or measles. My head turned heavy like a big rotten pumpkin. Then there were a dozen each of Pepper and the Map Man and they were all blurry. I felt like there was an oven on in my hair. Beers One, Two and Three and everything I had eaten since I was twelve years old rose suddenly from my stomach up through my throat toward my mouth.

I put both hands over my mouth, stood up as best I could and ran as best I could toward the back of the Buffalo Bayou Tap Room.

One of the Lillian-the-Come-Lady waitresses screamed, "Take a right at the light!" I had no idea what she meant and the first door I got open turned out to be the women's restroom. There were a couple of young ladies in there with their stockings down around their shoes and they yelled at me to get out of there. But when they saw what my problem was they shut up and ran out of there themselves. One of them even left open the door to the first stall and that small act of kindness and care saved me no end of trouble.

My head barely made it to the front edge of the commode in time.

I thought my entire insides were coming up and out. I thought it would never end. I thought I would have TB or be like Dracula or Frankenstein forever after if they did. I thought the top of my head had flown away. I thought I had accidentally swallowed Pepper's dirty white shirt. I thought the Holy Roads had sicced God on me for stealing the *Russell's Official National Motor Coach Guide.* I thought the Texas Rangers had gotten me for stealing the little Red Rocket bus.

I thought I was going to die.

Through the haze came Pepper. He had a towel or folded paper or something that was wet and he kept wiping it across my forehead during breaks from heaving. "It's going to be all right, Mack," he said. "It's going to be all right, Mack." He must have said it a hundred fifty times. But I didn't believe him. I didn't think it was going to be all right ever again.

Whatever happened to the trooper's kid who called himself The One-Eyed Mack?

He drowned in a commode in the ladies' restroom at the Buffalo Bayou Tap Room in Houston, Texas.

Too bad. He wasn't even twenty and had his whole life ahead of him.

The next bus to Austin wasn't for another two hours so we plopped our things and ourselves off in one corner of the bus station waiting room. It was the largest bus station I had ever been in. There must have been places for at least a hundred people to sit and wait, and the ticket counter had slots for five ticket agents and even that late at night two of them were open with agents on duty. There was a huge restaurant and a shop that sold cigarettes, newspapers and all kinds of candy, including Milky Ways. On one wall there was a map of the United States that was nearly as big as the front of our house in Kansas. The Continental Trailways routes around the country were marked in big red lines and the others were in small black ones. It took a while but I found Marion, Hillsboro and Goessel on there on black lines. Wichita and Newton, too, but they were on the red. And it was fun finding Austin and looking at where Galveston was and then Beaumont and Lufkin and Houston.

Hey, everybody! Look here at The Route of The One-Eyed Mack, America's newest and youngest and sickest drunkard!

The Map Man finally dozed off there in his waiting-room seat next to me. I was trying very hard to do the same, because Pepper told me my pain would be over and I would be my old self when I woke up. But I felt so bad it kept me awake, and I was only barely drowsing really when Pepper got up from his seat and said he was going to the bathroom and he would probably be a while, if I knew what he meant.

I started to close my eyes again and as I did I glanced toward the big main doors of the depot way on the other side of the room. I saw a man come through the revolving door who walked like Alan Ladd, my dad and the Map Man. Could there be a fourth guy in this world who walked the same way? What was Alan Ladd doing in the Continental Trailways bus depot in Houston, Texas?

This time it really was Dad. He spied me and without much of a change on his face he walked right on toward me.

Do I run to meet him? Do I hug him? Shake hands? Act like I have amnesia and don't know who he is? Run into the restroom with Pepper and lock myself in a stall?

"Hi, son," he said in that wonderful deep voice of his, just like he said it every afternoon when he got home from patrolling and I came home from school or from work on the county roads.

"Hi, Dad."

I stood up and he stuck out his hand and I shook it. I had forgotten how much taller he was than me. He was nearly six feet and I was only five-ten. That was because my momma was so tiny, just five feet tall and for some reason my Methodist God went with her instead of Dad on height. Meg got Dad's and she hated that because she was five-eleven. It never made sense or seemed fair to either of us.

"You left a pretty good trail, son."

"Yes, sir." Does he know about Gertrude the Flxible three blocks away? The *Russell's Official National Motor Coach Guide* burglary in Lufkin? Lillian the Come Lady? The lie to the Texas Chief conductor?

He was wearing his only suit, a dark blue one that Momma made him buy years ago. He wore it to church and to funerals and that was about it. The rest of the time he was in his Kansas State Highway Patrolman's uniform or in rough-around work clothes he picked up usually at J. C. Penney's in Hutchinson or McPherson.

I liked and loved my dad very much and I knew what he was going to say next and I had no idea what I was going to say back.

"Is that your stuff in your mother's old bag?"

"Yes, sir."

"Well, grab it and let's get on back. We'll catch the Texas

Chief streamliner and be back home tomorrow afternoon."

"No, sir," I said, as firmly as my quivering lip and spirit and soul would allow.

He sighed heavily and sat down in the seat on my left, where Pepper had been sitting before he went to the bathroom. The Map Man continued to snooze on my right. I sat back down.

"What is this all about, son?" He was clearly exasperated with me and mad and trying very hard not to show it. He crinkled his nose and sniffed the air a couple of times. "Is what I smell you or this seat?"

"The seat, I guess. Dad, I have a new friend who smells but he and I are doing some traveling and I'm 19 and a half years old and a junior college graduate."

"So I can't make you go home, is that it?"

"Yes, sir."

"That friend of yours? Where is he?"

"In the bathroom."

"Who did he tell you he was?"

"Well . . . why?"

"He's a wanted criminal, one of what they call the Bad Bowens."

"I don't know anything about the Bad Bowens." And I knew for certain that I didn't want to know anything and that he was now going to tell me anyhow.

"They're a whole family of crooks and outlaws that go back to Arnold Bowen, who used to hold up Santa Fe trains in the Panhandle in the 1890s. Your friend's daddy is at Leavenworth serving a life sentence for bank robbery, his mother is doing time at the Alderson Federal Pen for women in West Virginia, one of his two brothers was killed in an armored-car robbery in Kentucky, and the other is off in Alabama probably doing state time for burglary and swindling or some other kind of crime. . . ."

"The Alabama brother writes newspaper stories about dead people."

" . . . Good. Your friend himself has several arrests for petty theft and small burglaries and trying to extort people out of their money and property."

"At least he hasn't done anything really serious."

"Not until last week, he didn't. He squeezed his way through and out a window of a small county jail west of Fort Worth. That's where he'd just come from when he got on the Texas Chief with you. Isn't that where you two met up?"

"Yes, sir. What would you do if he came walking in here from the bathroom?"

"Well, I'd be duty-bound to arrest him and hold him for the Houston police on charges of escaping from jail."

"I really don't want you to do that, Dad. Please don't. He's really a great guy, he really is. He and I have become very good friends. . . ."

He was doing his best to hold down his voice and his temper but I could tell they were both about to give way. "How can you call a man like that your friend? You were somebody who wanted nothing more than to be a lawman, and to hook up with a no-good runt crook is more than I can understand."

I thought of the Trooper Dream that was no more.

I wondered if Dad had ever had a friend he would give up his big toe for? Did he have a friend who would wipe the steering wheel of a little Flxible bus clean of his finger-prints?

I stood up.

"What if he did not come walking out of that bathroom door before you left here for the train station, what would you do?"

"I'd do nothing if I left here with my son."

"You wouldn't go in there and get him?"

"No, son, I wouldn't."

"You wouldn't call the Houston police?"

"No."

"Let me go say good-bye."

"Sure."

My headache and my awful-tasting mouth and my fever had all gone away the second I spotted Dad coming through the revolving door. Now, as I walked slowly to the men's restroom back behind us on the opposite side of the room, they all came back. But the second I pushed open the swinging door and stepped into the bathroom they were gone again.

"Hey there, Pepper!"

"Hey there, One-Eyed Mack!" His voice came from about halfway down the line of closed stalls. It was one huge men's room with ten stalls and as many urinals and washbasins, maybe even more. I walked down to the stall where he was. I leaned over and saw all of the others were vacant. Great.

"Hey there, Pepper, what are you doing?"

"Hey there, Mack, what do you think I'm doing?" he answered from behind the wooden stall door.

"You spend more time on the can than anybody in the history of the states of Kansas and Texas combined."

"You spend less time on the can than anybody in the history of all the United States of America combined."

Sad but true. Oh, how sad. Oh, how true.

"My dad's out in the waiting room."

There was a fast, tense breath taken on the other side of the door. Then, "Trooper Dad?"

"Yes, sir."

"How did he find us?"

"He said we left a pretty good trail."

Pepper laughed. "I guess a guy with an eyepatch and a funny hat is pretty easy to spot."

"Yes, sir."

"He doesn't know about the bus, does he?"

"He didn't say anything about it so I don't think so."

"Good. You'll be all right then."

"What about Lufkin?"

"That doesn't even count. All we took was that dumb bus-guide book of yours. Who'll ever miss it or care? He wants you to go home with him, I guess?"

"That's it."

"Are you going to?"

"Yes, sir."

There were so many questions I wanted to ask. What is it like to have your father in prison? And your mother? Where did you get to be so smart? Why don't you change your life?

"We're going back to Kansas on the train," I said finally. "Stay in here until we're gone and then you can come out and get on the bus for Austin. It's due to leave in another thirty minutes or so now."

"Thanks, Mister One-Eyed Mack, but I won't be going to Austin."

"Yes, you are. You've got to take the Map Man to see the governor. You've got to."

"No way. Not now. No way."

"Look, I'm giving you the rest of my money." I took all I had out of my pocket, folded it up and tossed it like a wad under the stall door at his feet. "There should be over seventy-five dollars still there. I'm just keeping a couple of dimes for some Grapettes and Milky Ways."

"That's your money, so keep it. Remember the rule—you can only give away what you steal."

He kicked the money back outside the stall to me. I kicked it right back.

"We promised we would take the Map Man to Austin and he's holding us to it," I said.

"You did the promising, not me."

"We were partners. When one talks, he talks for both."

I could hear him breathing and thinking.

"Yeah, okay. I'll take him to Austin." I saw his hand take the money.

"Glory."

"Amen."

And suddenly I wanted to cry. It was the third time since I left Kansas that I wanted to cry. But this time was different from the other two.

"So long, then," I said, not crying for the third time.

"Yeah."

I was at the swinging door on the way out when he shouted: "You came out of this with a great story to tell the grandson!"

"Yes, sir."

There was the sound of a commode flushing and then of a wooden stall door flapping open and shut. I turned around to see the crazy, lying, smelly, wonderful little outlaw leaning over a washbasin. The water was on and he was getting some liquid soap on his hands.

"Hey, Mister One-Eyed Mack, who is the governor of Texas anyhow?"

"Don't ask me, you're the Texan." His hands were now

white with soap lather, and I couldn't resist saying, "You might want to wash under your arms, too. The governor of Texas might appreciate it."

"Whoever he is."

"Whoever he is."

I stepped again toward the swinging door but I took only one step and then made the biggest decision of my life. I came right back over to Pepper at the washbasin.

"I'll meet you in Austin," I said.

"When?"

"Tomorrow maybe or the day after."

"Where?"

"How do I know?"

"Make it the governor's office."

"That's a deal."

He stuck his right hand full of soap at me to shake but I passed up the opportunity. He was grinning from ear to ear. So was I.

"Let me have my money back."

"Indian giver." He wiped off his hands and reached in his pants pockets for the wad of my money. He handed it to me and I gave him back two five-dollar bills for his and the Map Man's bus tickets to Austin.

"Did Trooper Dad say anything interesting about me?"

"He said you were one of the Bad Bowens."

"You still going to meet me in Austin?"

"Yes, sir."

The Map Man was awake when I got back to our seats in the waiting room. Dad sat there listening while I told the Map Man that I was leaving him here, that Pepper would take him on to Austin by himself. He didn't look completely up at me but there was an ever-so-slight move of his head and I got a quick look at his eyes. They were the same dark blue color as on the Kansas state flag.

I shook his hand and he reached into his pocket, pulled out a map and handed it to me.

"It's a Texaco of Oklahoma," he said. "A Gosha."

I took it and said, "How much?"

"Free of charge. It's a gift from Gertrude and me for being such a nice young man."

Hear that, Trooper Dad? This crazy Map Man thinks your one-eyed son is a nice young man.

"Thank you, sir." I had a feeling it was the first map he had ever just given away to somebody like that. I was touched.

"The part on the east from Vinita down to Claremore is all that's missing. I kept it so I wouldn't ever forget it."

"Good. Thank you."

"You're welcome," he said to the waiting-room floor.

9
Glory

Dad tried his best to talk to me. On the walk over to the Santa Fe train station he brought up the Cardinals and Stan the Man and the Doaker and things like that. But I wasn't interested. So he told me Bad Bowen stories while we waited an hour and a half or so for the Texas Chief streamliner.

—The whole Bowen family descended on a laundry and dry-cleaning place in Roswell, New Mexico, and held shot-guns on a dozen or so employees while they washed, cleaned and pressed every stitch of clothes the Bowen family owned.

—Pepper's mother, Charlene Wilma (Kerr) Bowen, was arrested in the act of holding up a post office truck in Cabool, Missouri, and claimed to the postal inspectors later that all she wanted were stamps to send letters to her husband, who was already at Leavenworth.

—Pepper's daddy, Henry Lester Bowen, was arrested the last time after he and a cousin of his named Wendell Bowen tried to hold up a bank in Sherman, Texas, where two federal bank examiners were holding a regional seminar on how to detect bank embezzlements. The examiners knew how to sound an alarm in a hurry and the two Bowens made it only to Denison, birthplace of General Dwight David Eisenhower, eleven miles away, before they were apprehended.

—Pepper's brother Henry Lester Bowen, Jr., died in a shoot-out with police after he and an uncle, Will Joe Bowen, and two other men dressed up in clown suits to hold up an armored car making a cash pick-up at a circus in Somerset, Kentucky. Somehow the police had been tipped off and were waiting for them. Pepper's brother was the only one killed.

Dad was a pretty good storyteller and, at any other time and if the stories involved somebody else's family besides Pepper's, I'm sure I would have loved them all. But not then. Dad could not understand how a Bad Bowen could be my friend and that made me angry and silent.

I had never been that way with my dad.

He finally gave up trying to talk to me about five minutes out of Houston. After that there were only three brief conversations.

North of Brenham, he said, "Your sister has been crying her eyes out since you ran away."

"I didn't run away, I went away."

"What's the difference, son?"

"Plenty, sir."

South of Cameron, he said, "I talked to the county about taking you back on the road crew."

"Good."

"They will."

"Good."

Then as we left the Temple station after a crew change and a lot of delay, he said, "Where's the glass eye?"

"I threw it away."

"We'll get you another in Wichita."

"Yes, sir."

It was after two in the morning by then and the lights were down in the railroad car and Dad was finally sleepy. I played possum by closing my one eye and waited for him to close his two. Before long he was snoring as only he could snore. It sounded like an old Massey-Ferguson tractor whistling and sputtering and clanking around. I had forgotten how loud and awful it was. But I was glad for it because I knew he really was asleep.

I had always hoped snoring like that was not something God had in mind for me still to inherit from my dad. I didn't snore yet and I prayed God would probably end up giving it to Meg because she already had Dad's height.

All I had inherited from him so far was the Trooper Dream and that wasn't any good anymore.

I got up from my seat slowly like an Indian scout and worked my way to the club car. A colored steward was sitting in one of the overstuffed chairs, not quite alseep. He hustled up a piece of Sante Fe Railroad stationery and a fountain pen and told me to go to the end of the club car, turn on a light and write what I needed to write there at one of the card tables.

I knew what I wanted to say and I wrote it quickly.

Dear Dad,

I am not ready to go home yet. There is a lot more I want to do first. Please do not try to find me or worry about me because I will be 20 in July. Tell Meg not to cry too long. I will be in touch, I promise.

Your loving son.

I went back to our car, sat down and watched Dad sleep as I waited for the next stop to come. It was Hillsboro, Texas. Just a minute or two before the train came to a complete stop I stuck the note into the lapel pocket of his blue suit coat. Then I grabbed my white Roebaugh-Buck's bag and got off the train, which stopped there for only a minute or two before sliding on away again toward Kansas and other points north. It was a diesel but way back at the end of the train where I got off I couldn't hear a sound. It was like it was a glider.

Hillsboro, Texas. By an outside light on the train station platform I looked it up in my *Russell's Official National Motor Coach Guide*. It was served by Southwestern Greyhound Lines, and if I was reading the schedules right, there would be a bus through here to Austin in another two hours. The night agent at the train station told me how to get to the drugstore where the Greyhound stopped. It was seven blocks away and it was closed, but I didn't care. I sat down on the curb in front.

Whatever happened to the trooper's son who used to dream the Trooper Dream?

He got off the Texas Chief streamliner at Hillsboro, Texas, and went on toward Glory.

The Greyhound bus was a *Queen Mary* luxury liner compared to Gertrude. It had fancy silver on the sides outside and all kinds of blue and gray and silver things inside. The driver was also in blue and gray and silver, with a holstered ticket punch and creased pants and shirt and a hat with a shiny black bill which he wore like the Army Air Force pilots wore theirs in the war. He was what my Uncle Randy in

Chanute would have called a Kansas City Strutter, a fancy-dan starting pitcher.

I stepped up and inside his bus to a wonderful adventure smell of cigarettes and hair tonic and magazines. Only a few overhead lights were on and I suddenly felt like I was going on an important, dangerous mission and the driver was the commando captain played by Randolph Scott who would lead me to Glory.

Two hours later I got off the bus in Austin feeling like at least a million dollars. Except for my stomach. It ached badly. Bad Bowen badly.

I saw the State Capitol of Texas the second I stepped outside the bus depot. There it was to the right at the top of a hill at the end of the main street. Eight, maybe nine, blocks away. It looked huge, permanent, a giant double-jumbo version of the county courthouse in Lufkin.

I moved up that hill as fast as my hurting stomach would allow.

There was a Kansas-y north wind blowing into my face, through my clothes and under my skin, but I barely felt it.

I was hot to get up there and on to Glory.

It had been six days since I left home on the Santa Fe doodle bug for Newton and pirate points south and I still had not moved my bowels. I know it is not something people are supposed to talk about except to mothers and school nurses, but it had become a very serious problem. I knew beyond a doubt as we walked into the State Capitol of Texas that either I solved the problem pretty soon or my exciting new life was going to be a misery.

Why did you come home, son?

I had to go to the bathroom, sir.

119

How long has it been since you went, son?

Six years, four months, ten days, three hours and five minutes, sir.

My grandmother Lardner, who died of pneumonia while visiting her sister in Great Bend, used tons of Ex-Lax and prune juice to overcome her irregularity and I thought maybe that was where I would probably have to turn, too.

Pepper, the Map Man and I were walking up the huge steps toward the governor's office on the second floor when I decided to ask Pepper for some advice on the matter. I had found the two of them at the first-floor information desk. He had just told me how it was not in his family tradition to walk voluntarily into government buildings and he was feeling a bit uneasy about it. He said the marble floors made it worse because even hard rubber-soled shoes sounded like a battalion of Texas Rangers were coming down the hall to get him.

His advice for solving my problem was: "Think you're someplace else, someplace magic, someplace that makes you feel good and relaxed and happy. That's what I always do and that's why I can go anytime there's the slightest message of need. It's mental, not physical. That's what people don't understand."

Thank you, sir.

And we arrived at and entered the Governor's Reception Room.

The room smelled like the lobby at Farmers and Drovers State Bank and was almost as big as the Santa Fe railroad station in Galveston. The ceiling was higher than most trees in Kansas and there were oil paintings of Texas governors on the walls and fancy, overstuffed chairs and couches around for people to sit in. I had never been in any place so nice.

I wondered if you had to have two eyes to be governor of Texas. How about lieutenant governor?

We had no plan, no scheme. So we just walked up to a lady behind a desk. She was about thirty and was pretty. Pepper and I were on each side of the Map Man, who kept his head down so he could stare at the pretty lady's fingernails.

"Could you please tell us the name of the governor of Texas?" I said in as quiet and dignified a way as I knew how.

The lady took a sniff of Pepper on the other side of the Map Man, frowned and then almost smiled. It was clearly part of her job to almost smile at everybody who came in there.

"You must be the only three people in Texas who do not know the governor is Allan Bernard Shivers of Woodville," she said.

"Woodville?" I said with great cheer and happiness. "We went through there a couple of days ago on the Texas Red Rocket bus from Beaumont to Lufkin. Isn't that an amazing coincidence?"

"We would have looked him up if we had known," Pepper added.

"The governor does not live in Woodville anymore. All governors of Texas live in Austin." Her tone was icy enough to freeze up the Arkansas River all the way from Wichita to the Oklahoma border.

"What do you call him for short?" Pepper said, and I wished he hadn't.

"We don't call governors of Texas anything except Governor for short," said Pretty Lady. "Now what can I do for you?"

It was obvious she didn't want to do anything for us, but

she asked, so we told her our friend in the middle here had a message for the governor. She said she would be more than willing to take it and deliver it to Mr. Shivers. The Map Man said that just would not do, because of Gertrude. He said he had promised Gertrude he would deliver it in person and he had never broken a promise to her in his life and he wasn't about to start now.

Pretty Lady said that was what we all would call a Nasty Break because there was no way the governor was going to see any or all of us this fine day.

Pepper told her we'd just wait here until tomorrow then. Pretty Lady, her nose still picking up his smell directly and smartly, was obviously mortified and sick at such an idea. I said in a stroke of pure pirate genius, Yeah, we'll make ourselves comfortable on that couch over there. She looked at that couch with panic in her eyes, like the priceless thing would surely have to be burned afterward like they do the clothes of people who catch diphtheria.

"Wait here," she said, standing up. "Wait right here at the desk. Don't move. Don't . . . don't even sit down."

"Yes, ma'am," I said.

She returned in only a minute or two with a tall, handsome man about Dad's age with combed-back black hair. He was dressed in a white shirt and blue and red tie and shiny brown loafers. His right hand was out in front of him and he was smiling.

"I'm Allan Shivers," he said in a voice that was twice as deep as Dad's, which meant it was deeper than any other voice I had ever heard except on the radio. "Which one of you has a message for me?"

We all kind of steered him toward the Map Man, who

raised his head long enough to make connections between his right hand and the governor's.

"What can I do for you?" said Mr. Shivers, like he really cared.

"It's Gertrude," said the Map Man to the floor.

"What about her?"

"She's very sick."

"I'm sorry."

"She wants me to tell you she is so sorry."

"For what?"

"For stealing Cecilia Ann Abernathy's, her best friend's locket."

"Where did it happen?"

"In Lufkin, Texas."

"Angelina County, I know it well. When?"

"Nineteen twenty-seven. May nineteenth. It was just lying there on her dressing bureau and Gertrude took it and put it in her pocket. But she never wore it."

"Has she told Cecilia she's sorry?"

"She can't find her and I can't either."

The governor took a step back, took a deep breath and in a voice as deep as the Holy Road God, said: "By the authority vested in me as the governor of Texas, I hereby pardon Gertrude . . . what's her last name?"

"Williams was her maiden name. Her father was Herbert Denton Williams. . . ."

"I hereby pardon Gertrude Williams, daughter of Herbert Denton Williams of Lufkin, Angelina County, Texas, for stealing her friend Cecilia's locket on May nineteenth, nineteen twenty-seven."

Mr. Shivers, who I liked right then more than anybody in

the world, shook the Map Man's hand again, smiled at me, sniffed and frowned at Pepper and disappeared through a door off to the left somewhere.

Back at the bus station a short while later, I went directly to a middle stall in the men's room and followed Pepper's advice. I kept my mind only on that wonderful, magic, beautiful, happy thing that had just happened in Governor Allan Shivers's wonderful, magic, beautiful, happy reception room.

And found Glory.

We got off the bus in Joplin, Missouri, and in only a few blocks and minutes we were walking up a long brick sidewalk through some high shrubs and bushes to the front door of a big gray and black and white house. The mail box had the name Marshall M. Mooney on it.

The Map Man had raised his head and had been looking straight ahead since we got off the bus.

He left Pepper and me in a downstairs parlor for a few minutes while he went upstairs. Then he came and took us up for a peek at Gertrude. She had a gray face and red eyes and was about as close to being dead as I had ever seen an alive person. I'm sure Momma must have looked about the same right before she died but I was not allowed to see her so I don't know. Dad said she was unconscious and there was no point in my remembering her that way.

Pepper and I got only one short, sad glimpse of Gertrude. A nurse and a woman friend who were there said she spent most of her time under an oxygen tent asleep and spoke only occasionally. But they said Gertrude opened her eyes and smiled when the Map Man came into her room, and she said, "Thank you, dear boy," when he told her about what he had said to the governor of Texas and what the governor had done. The woman friend said Gertrude always called the Map Man "dear boy," even though he was her husband.

The Map Man took us next to a basement room to see his maps. It was unbelievable. The room was nothing but maps. He had cardboard box after cardboard box of them sorted and arranged alphabetically and by kind and publisher and year. There was a section on countries, another on cities and towns, another on states, another on counties. Most were from Skelly, Texaco, Humble, Standard, Derby and other oil companies, but there were also stacks of road atlas books and pamphlets that stores and other businesses sold or gave away. The walls of the room were covered with big framed maps, the biggest being a 1916 Shell of the state of Missouri. The second biggest was a 1922 National Geographic of Kansas City, Missouri and Kansas, together, and the others were of downtown St. Louis, Angelina County, Texas, and Boone County, Missouri.

Everyone of them had a corner section torn off.

Marshall M. Mooney, the Map Man, must have been a prominent man of Joplin. There was a bookcase of gavels, like judges and chairmen of Rotary Clubs use, and photographs of him standing in front of fancy buildings and new cars and sitting at fancy tables and desks. There were also several engraved silver trophy cups and platters and bowls on a mantel.

There was a stuffed head of a deer over the mantel. I had seen pictures of stuffed deer's heads before but I had never seen a real one in person.

I couldn't even imagine what had happened to turn Marshall M. Mooney into somebody who never looked up, who collected maps and tore corners off of them and who went off to Texas to make amends for his wife's having stolen a locket more than twenty years before. My Uncle Randy, the one in Chanute, said some people just wake up one morning out of their minds for no particular reason. I was seven years old when he told me that, and most mornings afterward, until I was fifteen, I woke up wondering if this was the morning for me. Maybe it happened that way to Marshall M. Mooney. Maybe Gertrude's dying drove him out of his mind.

Maybe it was none of my business.

"She is determined to balance what she calls her humanity books before she dies," whispered the woman friend at the door of a third-floor bedroom where she had insisted Pepper and I stay the night. "Poor Marshall has been everywhere trying to find people she remembers doing terrible things to years ago. It's so terribly sad."

"Yes, ma'am," I said.

"Thank you so much for bringing Marshall home."

"It was our pleasure," said Pepper.

"I just hope she doesn't send him off again. The doctors don't think she has more than a few weeks left now."

Pepper and I didn't say much of anything to each other for a while. I very much wanted to cry but that was out of the question.

Finally he brought up where we were going next.

"Leavenworth's not that far north of here, how about going by to see my dad, Big Bo Bowen?" he said. "He doesn't bite anymore."

"Fine with me," I said. And that was that.

Then I brought up his smell. I just had to. The trip up from Austin had been awful. On the Dallas–Tulsa overnight leg I was right there with him and between his putridness and the chorus of honks and wheezes from the other sleeping, snoring passengers I thought I was on the Holy Road to Hell.

"It's the smell of dead buffalo," he said, like he was telling the truth. "I inherited it from Great-grandfather Bowen, who stole and slaughtered so many buffalo in Colorado and western Kansas it got into his genes and it got passed on to me."

"Liar."

"I would remind you, too, Mister One-Eyed Mack, that if it hadn't been for my stink, Governor Allan Bernard Shivers would never have pardoned Gertrude and we'd still be back in Austin trying to figure out something."

"You take a bath tonight or I'm not going to Leavenworth," I said, half afraid he'd say, Okay, fine, see you in the next life.

"Okay, fine," he said. "See you in the next life."

We each had a twin bed and they were a good ten feet apart. He turned over in his and soon I heard him snoring just like Trooper Dad did and the passengers on the bus had the night before.

It was a long while before I fell asleep.

Morning came and Pepper was sitting fully dressed on the edge of my bed. He reeked of L-A-V-A, just like in Lufkin! Was I dreaming? Was I awake? Did it really happen?

Yes, yes, yes. Glory, Glory, Glory in the Highest. He had bathed!

But there was a catch. The very worst kind of catch.

"I'm out of money," he said. "I don't even have enough for the bus ticket to Leavenworth."

"I've still got enough for both of us."

"Nope, I want my own."

An hour later we said our good-byes to the nurse and Gertrude's woman friend at the front door. They said Mr.

127

Mooney had already gone out but they didn't know where, or when he would be back. We told them to please give our best to him and to Mrs. Gertrude Mooney. We walked down the path to the sidewalk and turned right toward the bus station.

A silver Kiwanis Club bowl from the mantel was in Pepper's satchel.

A silver trophy cup from a Joplin Country Club golf tournament was in the bottom of my Roebaugh-Buck's bag down with the *Russell's Official National Motor Coach Guide.*

Pepper said stealing was the only way in the world he knew how to get money. He said nobody would ever miss or care about what we had taken. He said even if we did get caught it would be a first offense for me, and anyhow all I had done was stand watch while he took the two things and then allowed him to put the trophy in my bag.

I told him this was it for me. This and only it. Never again. I told him he was now going to learn how to work like normal people do and earn his money like normal people do.

He told me he wasn't sure he wanted to be a normal person.

I said either he promised to try or there was no deal, bath or no bath, L-A-V-A or no L-A-V-A.

He said, Okay, deal.

They should hang people for doing what I did and I was ready for it to happen.

We walked in the bus station and there sat Marshall M. Mooney, the Map Man, in the waiting room. I grabbed Pepper's arm to keep him from turning and running.

"Where you headed this time?" I asked Mr. Mooney.

"Paragould, Arkansas," he said, not looking at me, of course. "Gertrude remembered a cousin down there whose postcard from the Chicago World's Fair she never answered."

"When was that?" said Pepper.

"I don't know," said Mr. Mooney.

"We're headed north, the other direction," I said.

"Maybe next trip," Pepper said, who had a very strange look on his face. Like one of those crazy Holy Roads was yelling at him.

Gertrude might be dead when her loyal Map Man got back from Arkansas. Maybe she was keeping him on the go so he wouldn't have to be there and watch her die. Who knows? Whose business is it to know besides theirs?

The PA announcement for his bus was made: "All aboard for Sante Fe Trailways ten thirty-five A.M. Thru-Liner to Monett, Eureka Springs, Branson, Clinton and Little Rock and points south and east."

Mr. Mooney got up and so did Tom Bell Pepper Bowen.

"Mister Mooney, I have a confession to make," said Pepper. "I stole two of the silver things from off your mantel. One of them is in my suitcase here. The other's in Mack's sack."

Glory.

"I am very, very sorry."

Glory, Glory.

"I am going to go back to your house and put them back where they belong. Will you forgive me?"

Glory, Glory, Glory!

The women at the house didn't know or care what we were up to when we came back and said we thought we might have left something in the living room. We put the Kiwanis bowl and the Joplin Country Club trophy back where they belonged and left again for the bus station.

I told Pepper how proud and happy I was about what he had done.

"New rule, Mister One-Eyed Mack. Never steal from somebody you know and like," he said.

"You ever given anything back like that before?"

"Nope. Never wanted to."

"I guess this is what the Holy Roads mean by Glory," I said.

"I guess."

Our bus north left twenty minutes later. It was operated by a company called Crown Coaches. The bus was blue and white and was made by General Motors like the big Greyhounds but I had never seen one exactly like it before.

"Want to pirate one and drive it to Leavenworth?" I said to Pepper just before we got aboard.

"Are you serious?"

"No, sir."

It was the truth. I thought.

10
Love and Leavenworth

The only serious conversation I had had about girls was with a counselor at Brady Bruce YMCA Camp when I was thirteen years old. And it wasn't really about girls.

The camp was over in southeast Kansas between Parsons and Iola. It was named for Brady Bruce, a soldier from Parsons who died in the second wave of the D Day invasion in France. I went to it only one summer and that was because Uncle Charlie paid for it as a birthday present.

The counselor was a college shortstop type who went to Kansas State Teachers at Pittsburg. He told us the first night it was part of his responsibility as cabin counselor to check our sheets in the morning for wet dreams. He said if any of us had any questions about them now, he would be more than happy to answer them.

Nobody had any questions about them now.

But three mornings later he checked the sheets and found that several of us campers—including me, I must confess—had had a wet dream. He said there would be a Wet Dream

Meeting that evening after chow, which was what they called meals at the camp. Attendance was mandatory.

The guy was very serious about it. He started the meeting by explaining where the wetness comes from, which I appreciated. Then he told us why it comes, which I appreciated even more. His big pitch was that it was perfectly normal.

"All males of all sizes and ages and persuasions have them," he said.

"Baptists?" asked a kid from Iola.

"All religions," the counselor replied. "Even Catholics."

"My mother doesn't think it's so normal," spoke up a kid from Chanute. "She cries every time she finds my sheets wet."

"My mother told me to quit blowing my nose on the sheet," said another kid from Chanute. "She doesn't even know what's happening."

"She probably thinks you're masturbating and doesn't wish to embarrass you by talking about it," said the counselor, like he was talking about the Cardinals' won-lost record for 1948.

"Oh," said the second kid from Chanute. I could tell he was really glad after all that his mother had decided not to talk about it.

The counselor then went into the voice he was obviously working on to use when he graduated from K-Teachers and became a high school track coach and biology teacher.

"Let me tell you a fact," he said. "Some of the most prominent and important men in this world have had or continue to have wet dreams."

"Name one," said a kid from Wichita.

"General Dwight David Eisenhower," the counselor said, like he was announcing the End of the World.

"What about Roy Rogers?" yelled the first kid from Chanute.

"Him too. You bet," said the counselor.

General Dwight David Eisenhower! Roy Rogers!

That pretty much ended my only serious conversation about girls and did away forever with any concerns I had about wet dreams. I relaxed and enjoyed them and that was fine. But that was about all there had been, not counting what happened with Lillian the Come Lady on The Beaumont Rocket.

I had kissed two girls twice each but had never touched a girl's person except on those four occasions, and a couple of other times when I held hands. It wasn't that I didn't want to do things with and to girls, it just wasn't in the cards. Particularly after I lost the eye. Most particularly after I got the glass eye. Most, most particularly after Willie Allen McDaniel and Sammy Pardoe told everyone in school a bad case of gonorrhea had caused my left eye to disappear. They meant it as a joke, of course, but some of the girls didn't take it that way.

Lisa Andrews, the Miss Posture Perfect from my dying-on-the-train-track dream, was the one who told me. She was one of the two girls I kissed, which happened on the Sophomore Day trip to Newton before I lost my eye. She barely spoke to me after the eye was gone and it was only on graduation day from junior college that she told me about the girls believing Willie and Sammy. Her last name and mine came next to one another in the alphabetical class list, so she had to walk into the gymnasium with me. It was during the hour or so we waited in line in our gowns outside beforehand that she told me.

Her breath smelled of some kind of liquor. They said it was champagne somebody had snuck over the line from Missouri. I was tempted to turn her in to Dad.

The reason for explaining all of this was Jackie, the most wonderful woman in the world.

She worked as a waitress in Martin's River Spot, a café just around the corner from the bus depot and around another corner from a Magnolia House–type hotel we were staying at in Leavenworth. Jackie was tiny, gorgeous and sharp, the kind of girl you had best not fool around with unless you are ready to see everything through to some kind of end.

Tom Bell Pepper Bowen was ready from the second he laid eyes on her, the second she came over to the two of us at the counter, the second she took our orders for coffee with cream and chocolate doughnuts.

So was I.

At first she flicked Pepper off like he was just another flea or fly, like she did three soldiers who were sitting at the other end of the same counter. But after a while I noticed her sniffing at Pepper and then frowning when she got close. She was interested.

I fell in love with Jackie at first sight as much as Pepper did. But just a minute or two after first sight I knew I was out of the running. She was at least twenty-two or twenty-three, to begin with, which made her too old or me too young, depending on how you wanted to look at it. And without any experience or training when it came to girls, much less to a real woman like Jackie, there was really no chance.

When I said she was tiny I meant she was about five feet tall. Her body was not tiny. It was like it was designed by the same people who made Coca-Cola bottles, with all of the sweeps and curves and lines just where they ought to be.

When I said she was gorgeous I meant it was impossible to keep my eyes off of her. Her hair was dark blond, cut short like one of Meg's most expensive dolls. Her skin was the color of a light mustard and smooth as Sherwin-Williams enamel. Her eyes were Greyhound light blue. Her nose was pointed perfectly like the air scoop on the rear of Gertrude and the other Texas Red Rocket Flxibles.

When I said she was sharp I meant she talked like she knew who you were and what you were up to before you even said a word.

I cannot describe exactly what it was like to just Thud! fall in love with her. I do not know why it was her instead of the other waitress at Martin's River Spot, who was a tall brunette who was also gorgeous and sharp. I don't know why it wasn't a girl on the bus from Joplin or a girl on the street in Austin, Texas, or whoever. Anderson, a guy at junior college, swore God managed a master list of girls guys were supposed to fall in love with. Otherwise, 150 would fall for the same one there, 2,150 for the same one there, none for this one and that, and it would be a sad mess.

Thanks a lot, Anderson. How come he put both Tom Bell Pepper Bowen and me on the list for the same girl?

It turned out Jackie was in Leavenworth for the same reason Pepper was. Her daddy was serving twenty-five to life for embezzling money from the bank he worked for in Illinois, then setting fire to the bank and its records to cover it all up, then wounding the FBI agent who came to arrest him and then, finally, escaping from the minimum-security federal prison in Texarkana where they had sent him first. She had come to live in Leavenworth so she could be close and see him regularly. Her mother was dead like mine.

Pepper introduced me to several family friends around town with similar stories. The woman who sold candy at the Kresge was the wife of Richard Allen Alden, the armored-car robber who after twelve years in prison still refused to tell where the $75,000 loot was or who was in it with him. A kid about my age who pumped gas at a Skelly station was the son of Mad Dog Becker, a guy who machine-gunned dead four bank employees and customers in Frederick, Maryland, because the bank president refused to pick up a ten-dollar bill that had fallen on the floor during the holdup. The mother of Darwin Hotback Sherman, the St. Louis gangster who liked to set people on fire and then turn his back on them while they burned, took tickets at the Worth Theater. His favorite aunt made the popcorn.

They all asked Pepper about Big Bo. Henry Lester Bowen, alias Big Bo, leader of the Bad Bowens.

We went to see him the third day we were in town. You couldn't just go up to the gate and visit somebody. It took some arranging.

Pepper walked into the prison like it was no big deal, like it was the bus station in Lufkin, the train station in Galveston or any other regular place. It was scary, monstrous, ugly to me. Even from the outside, the walls and the wire and the turrets and the guards and the guns and the gray made me shiver.

Inside it was worse. Nobody smiled, and the noises were all metal, and the smells were mostly of strong soap and cooking grease.

I had always liked guessing what people's parents looked like. Before I met him, I had Randy Martin Salisbury's dad pegged as a short man with no hair and a squeaky voice and that was exactly what he turned out to be. Same for his mother. Something caused me to think she was tall and beautiful like Alexis Smith and she was.

But I missed badly on Pepper's dad, Big Bo. I figured him

to be short and oily and skinny like his son. He was actually over six feet tall with Charles Atlas muscles in his arms and a beard on his chin. I also expected him to smell bad but instead he smelled like Lifebuoy.

The only two things they seemed to have in common was that they were kin and crooks.

"Pepper. My son, the Pepper!" he yelled when he walked into the visitors' room. He reached out like he was going to grab and hug and shake and do all kinds of loving, happy things to his son the Pepper. No way. There was a steel mesh there in the room separating the visitors from the prisoners. He sat down on a bench on one side of it. We sat down on the other.

"This is my friend, The One-Eyed Mack," Pepper said to his dad.

"Hi there, One-Eyed Mack," said Big Bo. He touched his right eye. "Some fed nick you?"

"No . . ."

"That's right," said Pepper. "A FBI man got him with a burst of tommy gun in Galveston. Mack had five grand he had just taken from the passengers on the Texas Chief."

Big Bo was delighted. "A train! You held up a train? Good for you. There's not enough of your kind around anymore. Hey, good for you, One-Eyed Mack."

"He also steals buses," Pepper said.

"What in the hell for?"

"Just to drive around in."

"Hey there, Mack, you are something," Big Bo said. Then he switched his attention to his son the Pepper. "What about you, son? Where have you been and what have you done since I saw you last?"

Pepper then told the longest continuous string of glorious

lies I had ever been a witness or an audience to.

"Well, first I went to work for the law as a hired vigilante for a sick sheriff in western Kansas. Then I went south and almost drowned in a hurricane while diving for Spanish gold in a shipwreck off the coast of Corpus Christi. Went back to Kansas next and worked for two weeks as an attendant to homicidal maniacs at the Kansas State Mental Hospital in Osawatomie until one of them tried to saw me in two with a coping saw and I quit. I fell in love and married and then divorced six weeks later a Sweet Sue of a little girl in Fort Worth who turned out to be an undercover Texas Ranger looking for leads about bank robbers. I followed in Sam's footsteps for a month or two and wrote dead-people stories and a high school football column for the morning newspaper in Beaumont, Texas. The sports bug bit me badly then so I spent the summer playing centerfield for the Boeing Bombers in the Kansas State Semi-Pro Baseball League in Wichita.

"And before coming here I was working for Governor Shivers of Texas as a personal advisor on criminal justice."

It was amazing the way that sea of lies flowed out of the mouth of the Pepper.

Big Bo loved it. He clapped and laughed and hooted and snorted through each and every entry. It was like Stan the Man Senior watching Stan the Man Junior hit 'em out of the park.

Whack! Look at my son. Whack!

Hit another one, son. Whack!

They were great together there, talking and joking around. Big Bo asked me some questions about myself and I told him about Trooper Dad. He got a kick out of a Bad Bowen being good friends with a trooper's kid.

After a while we ran out of things to talk about because

Pepper said beforehand not ever to bring up anything in the future. Big Bo was serving a life sentence and the chances of him getting out of there anytime soon were up there between slim and none. Pepper had also joked earlier with Jackie and me about helping both of their dads escape. He said only one guy had ever escaped from Leavenworth and he used Joe Palooka, Joe Louis, the Missouri Cavalry and the South Dakota Marines to help him. All Pepper lies. Joe Palooka was only a comic strip, Joe Louis was the heavyweight champion of the world, and I doubted if there were such things as the Missouri Cavalry or the South Dakota Marines.

It's not easy and there was a strain in talking only about the past and being careful never to say a thing about tomorrow, the day after, next week, next month or anything else in the future like that. I caught myself once, before I wondered if Stan the Man would hit the Cardinals to the World Series next year.

It was Big Bo himself who stopped the joking and funning around and broke the no-future-talk rule. And it changed my life.

He did it suddenly, like a black thunderstorm cloud had just come across his brain. "You know how long it's going to be before I get out of here, son?"

I had just been demonstrating Stan the Man's stance at the plate, the way he crouched and peeked out like around a corner at the pitcher, the way he twisted those hips just before the pitcher released the ball.

"Twelve years. That's minimum. That's if I keep my nose and my behind and my front clean. That's if I don't die from food poisoning, soap poisoning, lead poisoning, sugar diabetes, polio, cholera or spinal meningitis. That's if I don't burn up in a fire, if a brick doesn't fall on my head, if the Missouri

River doesn't flood and wash this prison and me away. That's if I get every break of every ball, every piece of luck, every everything good."

Pepper didn't say a word.

Neither did I. There was a part of me, though, that wanted to say: Hey, Big Bo, crimes does not pay. Didn't you know that?

"You know something else, son?" Big Bo continued. "You remember that Oklahoma grocery store holdup that went sour? The one in Muskogee with your brother Joe and Uncle Samuel? The one where the cashier happened to be a deputy sheriff on his day off with a shotgun under the counter? Well, Oklahoma's holding that warrant for me and Oklahoma says they want me when I'm through here and that's that. That means even if I get out of here in twelve years I go right into the Oklahoma state pen in McAlester. That's the worst thing, son. It takes all the fun out of counting off the time here. There's nothing to look forward to but another prison. I hate that, son. I just hate it. I try not to think about it but I do. I think about it all the time. I think, Okay, with everything right I got twelve more years and if I divide that into three four-year hunks for living and thinking purposes I can get through it. I'll only be fifty-two years old. Still time to get some things done, have some good times. Your momma is due out of Alderson in seven years so she'd only have to wait five more. Maybe we could move to the Missouri Ozarks where nobody'd know us. Buy a cabin down there by Eureka Springs somewhere. Open a hot-dog café that you can drive up to and be served, a Skelly service station or maybe even a linoleum-laying service. There's a guy in here who says there's money to be made laying linoleum.

"But then I think: Oklahoma! Oh, no! Oklahoma! I'm

going straight to McAlester pen! There'll never be linoleum. I'm never ever going to be free again. Oklahoma won't let me."

Pepper didn't talk for a long time. He just looked through the mesh at his father. His face was caught between sadness and a smile.

"What can I do to help you about Oklahoma?" Pepper asked finally. "Have you got a plan?"

"Nothing, except maybe you go and get yourself elected lieutenant governor of Oklahoma. A guy in here says it's a snap."

I expected Pepper to laugh. He didn't. In a deadly serious tone he asked, "Why lieutenant governor?"

"So you could pardon me for the grocery store."

"I thought governors pardoned."

I jumped in to say, "We know the governor of Texas. Shivers is his name. He pardoned a woman for us the other day."

"He can't help me in Oklahoma," said Big Bo. "The governor does actually do the act of pardoning but the lieutenant governor could get him to do it and it would be easier to get elected lieutenant governor."

"How easy?" Pepper asked. He was serious! I could not believe it.

"A guy named Morehead Allison is it now in Oklahoma. The guy here said Allison was just a county sheriff from way out in the Panhandle and decided one day he wanted to be lieutenant governor. Allison's a nothing guy. Ran one lousy jail. That's what made me think it must be pretty easy to be lieutenant governor."

"I couldn't just go to Oklahoma and become it just like that. You can't point a gun at somebody and steal it. 'This is a stickup, Oklahoma. I am now your lieutenant governor.' "

"No, no. You'd have to get into local politics somewhere small and local, I guess, and then tell 'em after a while you are ready to move on up to lieutenant governor. That's for you to figure out."

"I don't even know what the lieutenant governor of Oklahoma does."

"You got twelve years to learn."

"We'll think about it," Pepper said. Then he peeked around at me like I was the pitcher and he was Stan the Man. "What do you think, One-Eyed Mack?"

"I think you Bad Bowens are crazy."

Big Bo Bowen let out a happy whooping yell. Then he said, "What could be greater than the son of a Kansas trooper and the son of a man at Leavenworth teaming up like you two? It's the melting pot.

"It's America."

Lieutenant governor of Oklahoma?

It was one thing to go off to Oklahoma and become the lieutenant governor to help your dad but another to leave behind the girl you loved to do it. Pepper was in agony.

We walked across the Missouri River bridge from Leavenworth and dry Kansas to a tavern in wet Missouri. It was called The Show-Me Blue Moon. Pepper said he needed to hang a beer because it was his whole life he needed to think and talk and decide about.

We each ordered a Bud and a package of Tom's salted cashews. And there before me on the wall was another one of those huge pictures of Custer's Last Fight. I tried to imagine how many copies Budweiser must have had printed up. I tried to think about that meeting at Budweiser headquarters where somebody in charge turned to a couple of thousand or so salesmen in Budweiser suits and yelled like a cheerleader: "I want one of those Custer pictures on the wall of every bar in the United States of America! Got it? Now go to it!"

I wondered if they paid bar owners to put them on the wall or if most thought Indians scalping soldiers was attractive enough to put there for free on their own.

"I cannot imagine going through life without Jackie," Pepper said to start off the conversation. "I love her so much it makes my legs ache."

"Why your legs?" I asked, trying to be sympathetic.

"Shut up."

"Yes, sir."

"This is love, Mack. I am telling you this is real love."

"You ever been to Oklahoma?"

"A hundred times. Maybe more. I cannot imagine going through life in Oklahoma without her."

"Has she ever been to Oklahoma?"

"I don't think so. Nobody from Illinois's ever been to Oklahoma."

"Maybe she won't want to go. Maybe she needs to stay here in Leavenworth because of her daddy."

"No problem," Pepper said, "No problem at all. Her dad's up for parole in six months. He's going back to Decatur, Illinois. He's going to live happier ever after in the flag-making business."

"Flag-making business?"

"Jackie's dad's uncle owns the largest flag factory in southern Illinois, and he is sick with TB and is more than willing for his ex-con nephew—Jackie's dad—to take it over."

"I wished I had a relative who owned a factory of some kind I could take over someday."

"You're a pirate, Mister One-Eyed Mack. Running factories is the dumbest, dullest work in the world compared to pirating."

"What do you know about it?"

"Everybody knows being a pirate is a lot more fun than owning a factory."

He started picking the label off his Bud bottle with his fingernails. I threw a cashew up like I was a circus seal and caught it in my mouth. He went over to see if there was anything to play on the jukebox.

I got up and looked again at Custer's Last Fight. I noticed for the first time a dead Indian down in the right-hand corner. He was nearly naked and he died with his right hand to his forehead like he really could not believe what was happening to him. I thought we were supposed to win this thing!

I went back to the table and sat down. Pepper was already there.

"Nothing but songs on that thing that make me think of Jackie," he said.

"Mr. Pepper, I think the only way to solve your problem is maybe to marry Jackie right now or forget her coming to Oklahoma and forget ever seeing her again."

"Marry her?" He looked at me like I was a lunatic, then frowned and went silent like he was dead.

We finished our Buds and cashews without saying another word about Jackie, Oklahoma or life, and walked out and back across the bridge to Kansas.

Pepper popped the question at Martin's River Spot the next day during the slack period between the end of lunch and

the beginning of supper. He asked Jackie to go with him to
the booth in the farthest corner away from everything. She
said something about how serious he looked and something
must be wrong and she didn't know he had any secrets from
The One-Eyed Mack.

She looked so cute. She had put a silver metal hair-brad
thing on each side of her head to hold her magnificent hair.
And it seemed like her uniform dress was cleaner and star-
chier than usual and that she had on more rouge and lipstick
than usual. Jackie was a knockout just normally, but duded
up she was like a movie star.

I wished it was me who was popping the question.

I sat at the counter at the other end of the place while they
talked. I looked only straight ahead at the Coke clock and
the electric Pepsi waterfall and thought about marriage for
a while.

I thought mostly about what Anderson had told me about
it. He was a butane-gasman's son from Newton who showed
up one day at our junior college. Nobody paid much attention
to him because he was mostly crazy and ignorant. I was the
only one who really got to know him much and that was,
like Randy back in high school, because of the St. Louis
Cardinals. I saw him carrying a comic book about the life
story of Harry the Cat Brecheen. I introduced myself as a
Cardinal fan but he didn't really know anything. He didn't
know where The Cat came in the starting pitchers' rotation
or that his hometown was Adabel, Oklahoma. He didn't even
know Enos Slaughter's wife's name.

I just shrugged and started to walk away but he wanted
to talk about why major-league ballplayers and all other people got married.

"You know what the best thing about getting married is?" he asked.

"No," I answered.

"It's that it means you can do all the dirty things without them being dirty anymore."

"Mmmmm," I said.

"There your wife is doing the wash or walking to the bathroom or cleaning some strawberries at the sink. Anytime you want to say something dirty you just can say it. Anytime you want to do something dirty you can just do it."

"Well, what do you know?" I said.

"Now none of this is on the list of what the preacher or your momma will tell you about the nice parts of getting married, but it's right up there near the top of the list," said Anderson. "It's in invisible ink maybe but it's there. Believe you me."

You can see why we thought he was crazy and ignorant.

Their wedding was really nice. Pepper got a Holy Road preacher to do it free in the living room of his own parsonage by telling him my father was a Holy Road missionary with the Zulus in Africa and knew how to speak Zulu with a click-click between words like the Zulus did. I bought six light-blue carnations for Jackie to hold and a yellow one for Pepper to wear in his coat lapel. Nobody was there except the three of us, and the preacher and his teenage daughter who was in charge of the music and who smiled like a dime-store doll the whole time.

The preacher asked Pepper and Jackie to repeat a string of promises which they both did with no problem. He pronounced them man and wife. They kissed like it was a movie and nobody was watching.

Then the teenage daughter leaned over and put the needle on a phonograph record rendition of "Sunshine, Sunshine in My Soul Today, Sunshine, Sunshine All Along the Way."

The whole thing didn't take six minutes.

11
Lieutenant Governor of Oklahoma

We had to choose the exact place in Oklahoma to go and settle so Pepper could become the lieutenant governor of Oklahoma. You would have thought we were figuring out where to spend the night. I had the old Oklahoma map the Map Man had given me and we spent a good half-day looking at it. But Pepper was the only one who had been to anywhere on it. I had made only that one trip through Oklahoma on the Texas Chief streamliner in the middle of the night. Jackie hadn't even been close to Oklahoma and didn't know for sure where it was.

"I just want it to be someplace where there's no dust," she said. "I hate dust and Momma always said Oklahoma has too much of it."

That meant western Oklahoma was out.

"I don't want anyplace too big," I said. "No cities where you can't walk to most places and where the water tastes treated."

That meant no Oklahoma City or Tulsa.

"I don't want any small hick place where the next-door neighbor and the preacher and the librarian and the sheriff know everytime you don't feed the dog," Pepper said.

So it finally came to a place that wasn't too big, wasn't too small and wasn't dusty. Pepper said that brought it down to Enid, Muskogee, Lawton, Ponca City or Adabel.

Adabel? It had a sound to it I liked. Aid-ah-bell.

"What's Adabel like?" I asked.

"I've only been through there twice. Never stopped but I liked its looks," Pepper said.

"Why?" asked Jackie.

"Because everybody I saw on the streets was grinning like they just married the most beautiful girl in the world."

Adabel. We each said it a couple of dozen times. Adabel, Oklahoma. Adabel, Adabel, Adabel.

Jackie said it reminded her of "daffodil." It made Pepper think of Tom Bell Pepper Bowen.

" 'Who are you and where are you from, little man?' " Pepper said. " 'I am Tom Bell Pepper Bowen and I am from Adabel, Oklahoma.' "

"Well, I am Mrs. Tom Bell Pepper Bowen and I am from Adabel, Oklahoma, too."

It wasn't quite the same thing for me to say, "Hi, I'm The One-Eyed Mack and I'm from Adabel, Oklahoma." But I liked it. Particularly because it was Harry the Cat's hometown.

I used my own hot *Russell's Official National Motor Coach Guide* to work out our route to Adabel, Oklahoma. We would take a bus line called Don Lou Motor Coaches to Topeka,

Kansas, and then switch to The Thunderbird to go on south to Coffeyville, Tulsa and finally Adabel.

We got to the Leavenworth bus depot just after 6:30 in the morning and the Don Lou Motor Coaches bus was already there. Only it wasn't a real bus. It was a stretched-out car. Somebody had cut a Chevy in two and then welded a section of another car in between, with a couple of more rows of car seats.

The driver wasn't a real driver either. It was a lady. A tiny lady in black slacks and a gray blouse who was about the age Momma was when she died. Her hair was brown like hers, too, only tied up on the top of her head like Mrs. Williams's in Lufkin. If she'd been in a dress she could have passed for an English teacher.

"Who's Don Lou?" I asked all friendly.

"Don Lou is two people," she answered just as friendly. "I'm Lou. Don is my husband."

"What's he do?" Pepper asked, obviously wondering like me what kind of man he was not to be here driving this funny-looking bus to Topeka instead of his wife.

"He drives the Atchison run," she said. "It's east and up from here. He leaves at seven-fifteen."

Lou was tickled to discover Pepper and Jackie were newlyweds and I could tell she wondered who I was and why was I going off with them to settle in Adabel, Oklahoma.

I wondered that myself.

We were Lou's only passengers. Pepper and Jackie got in the first row of seats right behind her and I started to get in the row right behind them.

"Sit up front with me," she said. "It'll be cozier and we can talk."

I got in beside her and she pumped the accelerator and

turned the key and nothing happened. Like poor Gertrude the Flxible in front of the Buffalo Bayou Tap Room in Houston before her, she would not start.

Fortunately the loading dock at the bus depot was on a slight incline, so Pepper, Jackie and I were able to give a push to get the bus rolling well enough out on the street to get started.

Lou was furious. And a talker. A National League champion talker.

A World Series champion talker.

"I hate her and I love her," she said as we moved through the quiet streets of Leavenworth and on out of town. "I love her when she's running but I hate her like she is now. I just hate her. I keep telling Don she just isn't worth the trouble we go through to keep her running. She doesn't appreciate us. Can you imagine? Three passengers all the way to Topeka with a connection to catch and she won't start. She won't start! Can you imagine? Don says, Patience. I say, Patience, my foot. This girl is a loser. This girl is ready to be put to sleep. This girl is not worth the crying I do about her every day. Every day it's something.

"Today it's the battery. Yesterday it was the windshield wipers. You remember that gully-wash rain yesterday afternoon? We came back from Topeka in the middle of it—her and me—and suddenly without so much as a peep she stops the wipers. I couldn't see so I just pulled over to the side of the road until it quit raining. I sat there for thirty-eight minutes. Thirty-eight minutes! Does she care? No, siree. She comes right back this morning and decides not to start, with three passengers sitting up and ready to go all the way to Topeka.

"You want to know the awful truth? She wouldn't have

done it if the three of you hadn't been in here. She was punishing me. That's why we have to get rid of her. She holds grudges. I hate that in people and I hate that in buses, don't you? You've got to be able to move on in life or life will move on without you. Don't you agree? She can't get over the time we chose our other little bus, a 1943 Flxible, to carry a school group to Kansas City on a charter...."

"I knew a Flxible once," I said. "Her name was Gertrude."

"You know buses?"

"Yes, ma'am."

"Don and I were brought together by bus badges. You see that hat up there on the dashboard?"

I saw it. It looked like the regular black cap with a shiny leather bill that most bus drivers wear.

"You see that badge on the front of it?"

I saw it. It was a silver metal thing shaped like a police seal with a tiny red and white bus in the center and the words "Don Lou" engraved across the top and "Motor Coaches" across the bottom. Below that was the number 2. Was Don number 1?

"Don traveled for the company in Chicago that makes hat badges like that. They're the best in the business. There's another outfit in Providence, Rhode Island, that says they are, but Don's company really was. His sales territory was Missouri, Kansas, Oklahoma, Texas and Nebraska. He came to my town, Trenton, Missouri, to sell badges to the police department, the sheriff and to a little bus line that went over to St. Joseph. Henley-Shotwell Bus Line it was called. Mr. Shotwell—Phil Shotwell—had gone to high school with Daddy and they were best friends still. I was assistant manager of our telephone office and still living at home. We were all set to go over to the Shotwells' for dinner the same night Don had happened to pay a sales call at the bus line earlier in the day. Mr. Shotwell asked Don to join us.

"I don't know how love happened with your two friends in back, but Don and I had never laid eyes on each other before and we sat right there and fell in it while eating Mrs. Shotwell's meatloaf with green peppers and white onions, mashed potatoes, buttered carrots and pineapple Jell-O. Mr. Shotwell talked Don into going to work for him at the bus line, and a year later we were married.

"Five years after that we heard about this little bus line running out of Leavenworth to Atchison and Topeka like the Santa Fe Railroad began, and here we are. I guess you know the full name of the Santa Fe Railroad is the Atchison, Topeka and the Santa Fe? That's the answer to your question about how somebody like me ended up driving an awful little bus like this."

My question?

"I know you didn't really ask the question but you wanted to. Everybody does."

She took a breath, I took a breath. I glanced around at Jackie and Pepper. Their eyes were closed, which meant they were either asleep or playing possum. I couldn't blame them either way.

"Look at her!" Lou screamed. "She's been listening! She's punishing me again!" She meant the stretched-out bus.

Steam was blowing out from under the hood.

"It's not fair! I hate her! I am telling you, I hate her! Do you hear me, I hate this awful thing!"

Fortunately we were about to go into a town called Oskaloosa. In a couple of minutes we spit and chugged into a Derby Oil station. There was a young guy there with grease on his face and hands. He opened the hood, looked in and in a minute or two announced it was nothing serious and that it simply had overheated for no reason. He ordered us to sit for a while so the radiator could cool off until more water could be added.

"What did I tell you?" Lou said. "She's punishing me. She's the worst bus I have ever known. What was the Flxible like that you knew?"

"She was red and white and had an air scoop like an upside-down comma in the back. We called her Gertrude."

"I'd be ashamed to give this one a real name. I just call her Her."

It was such a relief to get on a Thunderbird in Topeka. It was a real bus, longer and larger even than Gertrude and the Flxibles. It was made by a company called Aerocoach.

Jackie and Pepper sat together in one pair of seats and I was across the aisle from them. Jackie had the window, and the two of them talked while I tried to daydream. It was very hard to do because Lou's voice was still whanging back and forth between my ears.

"... Phil Shotwell had gone to high school with Daddy and they were best friends still. . . . We were all set to go over to the Shotwell's for dinner . . ."

It was an hour or more after we said good-byes at the Topeka bus station before the sound went away completely.

Then I tried to bring up daydream pictures of me doing something in Adabel, Oklahoma.

Nothing came.

After a while Pepper suggested we see how many great Thoughts for the Week sayings we could make up for those signs outside churches. We had seen a couple of real ones in Yates Center, the last town we went through. They gave the name of the church, the hours of the services, the name of the pastor and a thought, like: "You'll Never Get A-Head If You Don't Have One."

"Man Who Lives by Bread Alone Is a Crumb," was Pepper's first.

I came back with: "Life Is Like Peanut Butter. It Goes Better Between Pieces of Love."

"Stand Tall for God or Sit Short for Good" was his next.

"A Lost Temper Is Never Found. A Found Smile Is Never Lost" was mine.

We went on and on with them and they got worse and worse. Jackie didn't play. She said she just wanted to imagine what Oklahoma looked like.

Pepper's worst was: "Give Your Heart to Jesus and You'll Never Have Heartache."

My worst: "Jesus Is the Light, You Are the Switch."

Finally Pepper said he had to rest and think some more about being the lieutenant governor of Oklahoma. He suggested he and I trade seats so I could come over and talk to Jackie for a while.

It was as we were moving from seat to seat that I noticed he did not smell anymore. It dawned on me that he hadn't smelled in several days. I couldn't quite remember the last time.

Had there been a Holy Odor Road miracle on the way to Glory?

"Where did your smell go?" I whispered to him as we stood in the aisle, changing seats.

"Love," he said.

"Love does away with b.o.?"

"That's it, Mister One-Eyed Mack. That's the lesson for the day."

"You are still the worst liar in this world."

"Ask Jackie."

I sat down next to Jackie. She smelled like flowers in a park. I wasn't about to ask her about the smell of her new husband.

We didn't talk about much of anything for the first thirty-five or forty miles. Mostly just about what we saw out the Aerocoach window. A few dogs, boys on tractors, women hanging out wash, hay bales, wheatfields cut down like they'd been given flattop haircuts.

"I'll make him do right, Mack," she said just after we left Fredonia, Kansas. "I know he's not used to doing right but he will now."

"No question, Jackie," I said. "No question." I told her about the silver Kiwanis bowl and Joplin Country Club trophy and how Pepper decided to give them back.

"That was like a revelation in church for him," I said.

"My daddy wasn't a crook all his life. Pepper doesn't have to be either," she said. "Daddy did his good part first and then did the bad. Pepper will just do it the opposite. He's been bad, now he'll be good."

"Yes, ma'am."

"I don't want any children of mine to grow up with their daddy in prison, Mack. I did that and there is nothing worse than that except being dead. Nothing at all worse."

"I believe you."

"Do you realize that I have known that man across the aisle that I am married to for only seven days? Seven days to the day this day."

"I've only known him twelve and the first two really don't count."

"I loved him the second he came into the café. I remember

157

it like it just happened two minutes ago. I saw him there at the counter and I knew. He saw me and he knew. Strange how that happens, isn't it, Mack?"

All I could think about was what if she had seen me at the counter and knew? Would her love have brought back my left eye the way it got rid of his smell?

I knew what I had in mind but I did not know what I was doing. I knew I chose that particular route from the *Russell's Official National Motor Coach Guide* because it would take us right through my Kansas town. I knew that the Thunderbird Aerocoach we were on was going to come right down Cottonwood Street past Carrie National Memorial High School, turn right on Poplar at the Skelly station, left on Ash at the Western Auto and come up the Alley between *The Pantagraph*'s newspaper office and the Rexall to Terrible Junior Dillard's Thunderbird bus depot.

I knew it was Wednesday morning, which meant Meg would be in a teller's cage at the Farmers and Drovers four blocks behind us on Locust. I knew Trooper Dad would be in traffic court at Emporia, eighty miles away.

I did not know if I was going to get off the bus. I did not know if I was going to stay off if I did. I did not know what I was going to say to Pepper and Jackie if I did stay off.

I did not know if I would go to the bank first or just walk to my house and wait for Meg and Dad to come home. I did not know what I would say to them when they did get there. I did not know if I was returning home for good or just for a visit.

I did not know what I was doing.

Through the bus window I could see that Terrible Junior Dillard was not inside behind the ticket counter. There was a young two-eyed guy in a crew cut selling tickets. He should have been me. I should be him. But if that was true then I would have never gotten on the Santa Fe doodle bug, the Texas Chief, Gertrude the Flxible or anything like them. I would never have gone to Galveston, Beaumont, Lufkin or Houston, to Austin, Joplin, Leavenworth or Topeka.

And I would never have met Pepper, Jackie, Big Bo, the Map Man and poor Gertrude the Woman, Governor Shivers of Texas, Lou of Don Lou Motor Coaches, Lillian the Come Lady and all the rest.

The driver had already gotten off the Aerocoach and gone inside the depot.

I made a decision. I stood up in the bus aisle. "I'm going inside a minute to get a Milky Way," I said to Pepper and Jackie. "They're my favorites and they may not have them in Oklahoma."

"Get me a pack of root beer Life Savers," Pepper said.

"I'd love a Butterfinger," Jackie said.

"Why are you taking that with you?" Pepper said, pointing to the white Roebaugh-Buck's bag I had taken down from the overhead luggage rack.

"Grabbed it out of habit," I said, putting it back. Good-bye, old sweet white bag. Good-bye, dirty clothes. Good-bye, *Russell's Official National Motor Coach Guide*.

Good-bye, Pepper and Jackie. See you in the next life, Adabel, Oklahoma.

"I'll be right back," I said, and got off the bus and went inside.

The ticket agent looked like he didn't know a one-way ticket from a suitcase and probably couldn't have read a Russell's guide if his life and both of his eyes depended on it. You could have had me, Terrible Junior Dillard. You could have had The One-Eyed Mack working for Glory and The Thunderbird. You could have had the very best one-eyed bus ticket agent in the whole Sunflower State of Kansas. Maybe the best in all of America. Maybe the world.

I ducked out of the depot and into the Rexall next door. They had Milky Ways, Life Savers and Butterfingers. It didn't make sense but I went ahead and bought one of each. The lady behind the cash register who took my money looked at me like she might know me but then changed her mind. She knew me but the hat and the eyepatch threw her off.

Her name was Mrs. Doke. I played with her son Jimmy Dale Doke on our Carrie Nation Hatchets baseball team. He thought he was something special because he batted lead-off, but that was only because he was only about three feet tall, which meant he got a lot of walks. Could anybody stand a guy who thought he was a great baseball player because he got a lot of walks? Hits are what count. Hits. I tried bunting to get on and I tried choking the bat way up and punching it to right field and I tried it with my hands down at the knob and swinging away like Stan the Man and Jolting Joe DiMaggio. I tried everything. All Jimmy Dale Doke did was go up there to the plate and try to make himself as little as possible so he would draw four balls and a walk. I don't remember him ever getting a good clean hit. Not that I got that many myself. But at least I was up there at the plate trying all the time.

I decided not to say, "Hey, Mrs. Doke, what's the latest on Jimmy Dale?" because I didn't care to know or hear anything about him. The last thing I had heard he was off at the University of Kansas at Lawrence on a baseball scholarship. That was either a lie or stupid of the Kansas Jayhawks. Could anybody imagine giving a baseball scholarship to a three-foot-tall guy who couldn't do much more than get walks? But if it was true I certainly did not want to hear about it.

Mrs. Doke put the Milky Way, the root beer Life Savers and the Butterfinger in a tiny brown sack. I took it and went to the back where the magazines were. There was a man standing there reading *Esquire*.

"Aren't you the trooper's son who went away?"

It was Chester Lawrence, the old man who sold divans and overstuffed chairs at the furniture store. He thought he looked like and was a whole lot like Chester Morris, the greasy-haired tough guy in the movies who drove runaway gangster trucks down the sides of mountains, landed gangster planes with only one engine working and always rushed home from Lisbon, South America or prison to be with his dying mother or neighborhood priest. I loved Chester Morris almost as much as Stan the Man and Roy Rogers. I wouldn't have minded being him either.

"No, sir, that ain't me," I said, trying my best to sound like Governor Allan Shivers of Texas.

"Then who are you there in that hat and patch?"

"My friends call me Jack Armstrong."

"The All-American boy?"

"Yes, sir."

"My friends call me Chester Morris."

"The movie star?"

"That's right, son."

"Well, you sure do favor him, that's for sure."

He smiled as big a smile as I had ever seen a grown Kansas man smile. "People tell me that all the time." Nobody had ever told him that. I was the first one. That's why he was smiling. It had finally happened.

Chester Lawrence put the *Esquire* back in the rack and walked out of that Rexall like he was in Chicago, Joliet or some other big-time gangster place, and I felt like my Kansas town was already a better place because I had returned.

Paramount Pictures presents *The One-Eyed Mack* starring Chester Morris and June Allyson. The Story of a Retired Bus Pirate Who Goes About His Kansas Town Spreading Happiness and Joy.

I glanced through a *Popular Mechanics* and a new comic book of Jolting Joe's life story. I needed only a few minutes for the Oklahoma-bound Thunderbird Aerocoach to be good and gone.

I went back outside to the sidewalk of Cottonwood Street and started walking in the direction of my house.

"Hey, you there in the funny hat. What happened to your other eye?"

I turned around. It was Pepper. And Jackie. They were standing there with their suitcases and my white Roebaugh-Buck's bag.

"Where's my root beer Life Savers?" said Pepper.

"I had my heart set on a Butterfinger," Jackie said.

"How could you live your life without this bag?" he said, holding up Momma's old Roebaugh-Buck's.

"How could you just go away without saying good-bye or anything?" she said.

"You all go on to Adabel, Oklahoma," I said. "You're married, you don't need a one-eyed third person like me hanging on to you."

"Do you think I can become the lietuenant governor of Oklahoma without your help?"

"Sure you can. It's crazy anyhow."

"You're our best friend, Mack," she said. "Our only best friend. That's not crazy."

"You two are the only ones I got, too," I said.

"Then what's going on here?" he said.

I reached into my pocket and gave him his root beer Life Savers and her her Butterfinger.

Metro-Goldwyn-Mayer presents *The One-Eyed Mack* starring Chester Morris and Vera Ellen. The Story of a Retired Bus Pirate Who Went to Adabel, Oklahoma, to Help One of His Two Best Friends Become the Lieutenant Governor of Oklahoma.

Lieutenant governor of Oklahoma? It *still* sounded crazy.

12
The First Six Days

The dirt had turned red almost exactly when we crossed into
Oklahoma just south of Coffeyville, Kansas. And it started
raining then too. So everything was red. The mud was red
and so were the splatters on the bumpers and headlights and
fenders of all cars and trucks. But then, as if the Great Mud
Maker had gotten tired of red mud, it had all turned black
again. Now the splatters were black.

Now we were coming into Adabel, Oklahoma, hometown
of Harry the Cat Brecheen, hometown of a future lieutenant
governor of Oklahoma, his wife and only best friend.

"Isn't Adabel a strange name for a town, now that I think
about it?" Jackie said from across the bus aisle. We were on
The Thunderbird's Tulsa-to-Adabel Express in a bus that
was manufactured by The Beck Company in Sydney, Ohio.
It was smaller than the Aerocoach but larger than a Flxible.

"Adabel must be some person's name," I said.

"Hi, I'm Pepper from Pepper, Nebraska."

"Well, hello, I'm The One-Eyed Mack from One-Eyed Mackville, Louisiana."

"Nice to know you both. I'm Jackie from Jackie City, Arizona."

"Maybe Adabel will turn out to be a beautiful girl and she'll be at the bus station to meet us," I said.

Hello, I'm Adabel Oklahoma. Welcome to my town, One-Eyed Mack. I've heard all about you from a woman on The Beaumont Rocket. Will you marry me and become Mr. Adabel Oklahoma?

Sorry, ma'am, but I'm already spoken-for to be a town name in Louisiana.

Then came the Brother Walt sign. It was big as a building, twice as big, and then some, as three regular billboards. In letters at least ten feet high it said:

BROTHER WALT WELCOMES YOU TO ADABEL, OKLAHOMA

There was a giant head of a smiling man with rosy cheeks and big black-rimmed glasses painted in natural colors right above the letters. Brother Walt himself, for sure. A fancy-looking church building was painted below the letters. "Come See Jesus First at the First Church of the Holy Road, Adabel, Oklahoma," was written under the picture of the church building.

"Thank you so much, Brother Walt," said Pepper to the sign.

"Are there Holy Roads everywhere?" I asked.

"They're following you, Mack. They're everywhere *you* are."

I had a feeling Pepper, for once, had spoken the rock-solid truth.

*   *   *

The beautiful Miss Adabel Oklahoma was not at The Thunderbird bus depot to greet us and love me. Brother Walt wasn't there either. It was after eight o'clock in the evening and the only person there, besides a few passengers, was a middle-aged man behind the ticket counter. He was a Starch, like Adam Rogers Wilson, the president of the bank where my sister worked. One of the guys at Carrie Nation said Mr. Wilson was really a high-rolling embezzler who took the bank's money out at night and drove over the line to Missouri and spent it on blue-eyed, pink-legged women from Chicago and whiskey sours.

The Starch behind the ticket counter was two-eyed. I wanted to yell: Hey, Mister Two-Eyed Starch, here I am, the best one-eyed bus ticket agent in the states of Kansas, Texas and Oklahoma and maybe the world. A job, please.

We walked out of the bus depot onto the streets of Adabel, Oklahoma.

"Nobody seems to be expecting us," Pepper said. "Nobody seems to know I have come to be their lieutenant governor."

He was right. The people of Adabel, Oklahoma who chose to be out on their downtown streets on that particular April evening paid us no mind. They didn't even stop to notice the guy in the eyepatch and the funny hat. That was probably because it was dark and they couldn't make me out that well.

"How do you like it so far?" I asked Jackie.

"I hate it," she said.

"It's dark. How do you know you hate it?"

"It smells."

"That's alfalfa."

"It smells like green peanut butter."

Across the street was a movie theater. Next to it a hotel. Next to it a Rexall, a furniture store with only mattresses in its front window and then a bar called The Boomer Sooner. I wondered if it had put a Custer's Last Fight picture on its wall. We walked a block farther past two banks, the Carnegie Library like the one at home, the Oklahoma Power and Light Company, and then we stopped.

"Do you want to get back on the bus and keep going?" I asked.

"Yes," said Jackie.

"No way," said Pepper. "I smell Glory."

"It's green peanut butter," said Jackie. She had hold of his hand and was squeezing tightly.

A small boy about nine came by us on the sidewalk, smiled and stopped. "Are you Christians?" he said.

"Holy Roads," Pepper answered in a hurry.

"Good. They're the best kind."

He walked on and I wanted very much to get back on the bus. "Let's go on to Ponca City or one of those other places on the list," I said. "I don't want to live somewhere where little boys come up and ask you questions like that. He should be home memorizing Cardinals' batting averages."

"I smell Glory," Pepper said.

We spent the night at a hotel called Brown's, and the next morning early I went out to find the house where Harry the Cat Brecheen lived when he was a boy. The hotel room clerk, a normal-looking old man who asked me how I lost my left eye, gave me directions. "But he doesn't live there anymore," he said.

It was easy to find, just six blocks from downtown out toward the high school. You would never have guessed from looking at it that the best left-handed curveball pitcher in all of baseball came from it. The house was old, green and white, one story, with a front-porch swing, a black metal mailbox and a bed of white flowers that made it smell like perfume all the way to a brick sidewalk that ran by in front.

Anybody could have lived there. A two-eyed bus ticket agent. A waitress even, or a crook, a teacher, a county commissioner or a blacktop spreader.

I thought about going up there and knocking on the door. Hello, you don't know me but nobody throws a curve from the portside the way The Cat does, and I was wondering if you could give me a smile, or maybe even an old sock or something of his that might still be just lying around the house?

I thought about how lucky Harry the Cat was to be a baseball star on the same team with Stan the Man. His picture on bubble gum cards, his name said on the radio, his life story in comic books.

I remembered what my Uncle Wilson in Newton told me one Christmas we spent with him and Aunt Louise. He said the saddest day of his life was the day he turned forty because it meant his dreams about being a major-league ballplayer were finally, really, a hundred percent over. Up till then, even though he hadn't had a glove on his left hand or a hardball in his right since he was eighteen years old, that dream possibility was always there. Sometimes he was at the plate for the Cardinals in the seventh game of the World Series, sometimes it was opening day. Sometimes he batted left-handed, sometimes right. Sometimes he took the count down to 3 and 2, sometimes he hit the first pitch. Sometimes it barely cleared the fence, sometimes it sailed up, up, away and over the lights. But whatever, he always socked the big one that won the big one. He said daydreaming like that got him through his early worst dry, scorching days working on wheat combines out near Cunningham in western Kansas. It got him through Army boot camp at Fort Dix, New Jersey, and the Battle of the Bulge. It got him through fights with Aunt Louise and later with his boss at the feed and farm supply store where he had worked for years and still worked. It got him through everything. "When the going got rough I just closed my brain, turned on the cheers, grabbed a bat and hit one out," he said. "It always got better."

I used to hit 'em out in my mind just like Uncle Wilson. Kick-the-can took that away when I was sixteen and a half. Along with the Trooper Dream. Thanks a lot, Jimmy T.

I like your house, Harry the Cat. Good luck next season.

Thanks, One-Eyed Mack. You'd have made a great St. Louis Cardinal yourself.

I decided not to go up to the door.

The next day, our second day in Adabel, Oklahoma, we settled into a rooming house a few blocks south of the bus station. It was a lot like the one Pepper and I had spent the night in in Lufkin, Texas. The main difference was that there wasn't a strange old lady running this place like there was there. Our landlady here was only thirty-five or so and nearly normal. She reminded me a bit of my Aunt Sally Josephine Winter in Salina. Both she and my aunt, who was my mother's aunt really and just my great-aunt, were tall and skinny like KU basketball players and had voices like they sang in church, which both did. Aunt Sally Josephine was a Methodist. Our landlady, whose name was Mrs. Vera Mutter, was a Holy Road.

Pepper and Jackie had a room on the first floor with a bath down the hall that only five or six others used. I had a room up, up and away on the third floor where it seemed like I had to share the bathroom with most of Adabel, Oklahoma. It was like standing in line during the war for meat and cigarettes and nylon stockings. Sometimes I just went outside, down the street and around the corner to a Skelly Station. I couldn't take a bath there but I could wash under my arms and do everything else that really mattered.

On our third day in Adabel, Oklahoma, I went back to the bus station to offer my super skills as a ticket agent to Mr. Starch and The Thunderbird. I had spent most of the time since we got to Adabel studying my stolen *Russell's Official National Motor Coach Guide* so I would seem even more bus smart than I really was. Stand by, Starch, for the bus show of your life!

He didn't want to talk to me. He said there were no openings and none was expected anytime soon.

"Greyhound is named after my Uncle Albert," I said. "He started it."

"Greyhound is a kind of dog, young man."

"Yes, like my uncle's dog. His name was Grey. Albert Finemore Grey. My uncle, not his dog. The dog was gray like the color but his name was Northland. My uncle's partners thought it would be great to have 'Northland' painted on the side of their little bus company's buses. So they decided to call the bus company Northland Grey-hound for the dog and my Uncle Albert's last name. And that's how the first Greyhound company was born in Minnesota, lo those many years ago. . . ."

Pepper had done this to me. Pepper had made it possible for me to lie like this to perfect-stranger adults. I never did anything like this until I met Pepper. It started with the conductor on the Texas Chief streamliner. Please, God of

Glory and the Holy Road, please forgive me, is probably what I should have immediately said to the heavens after what I said to Starch. But I didn't.

Starch did not know what to do. So he just stared at me for the count of twenty or thirty.

"Come with me, young man," he said finally, and I followed him into a tiny office behind the ticket counter. He sat down behind a tiny desk. There wasn't any place for me to sit so I remained standing like he was the high school principal and I was in trouble.

"I do not believe your uncle founded Northland Greyhound Lines, young man," said Starch. "Why you have come in here like this and told such a story is more than I can fathom. You're not an Oklahoman, are you?"

"I am now. I live right here in Adabel, Oklahoma."

"What were you from before, young man?"

"Kansas."

"I might have known." He sighed like somebody had just told him it was going to rain again tomorrow for the three hundredth day in a row. "What do you know about making out a bus ticket, young man?"

"I know all there is to know," I said. "I know about O-W ones and twos, R-T fours and sixes. I know about how to use rubber stamps to fill in the names of the towns. I know about how to use a validator to stamp the back of the ticket. I know about how to read a tariff so you know how much to charge. I know how to make out a package express waybill to anywhere in America. I know how to check baggage. I know about saying, 'Thank you for traveling The Thunderbird,' to the customer...."

Starch looked at me like I was some kind of freak. Hey, everyone in Adabel, Oklahoma, come see and hear this one-eyed crazy man at the bus station! Come one! Come all!

Then he started asking me questions like they were peanuts and I was what he came to see at the Wichita Zoo, where I went once with my dad and sister when I was seven.

"How would you route a passenger from here to Texarkana?"

"Thunderbird to Atoka, Jordon Bus Lines from Atoka to Ida, Oklahoma, then Baum Bus Lines from Ida to Texarkana."

"To Dallas?"

"Thunderbird to Ardmore. Dixie Trailways to Dallas."

"Who has the shortest route from Tulsa to Kansas City?"

"Southern Kansas Greyhound."

"The longest?"

"Southwestern Greyhound to Joplin, Crown Coach to Kansas City."

"What company runs from Abilene, Texas, to San Angelo, Texas?"

"Sun-Set Stages."

"From Wichita Falls to Lubbock?"

"Texas, New Mexico and Oklahoma Coaches."

"From Wichita, Kansas, to Harper?"

"Bickel Bus Line."

Starch stared some more and said, "I've never seen anything like you before." He stood up.

"I'm hired?" I said.

"We still have no openings."

"But when you have one I'll get it?"

"I can not promise you anything, young man."

I walked toward the front door and then I turned around and yelled as loud as I could: "It's because I only have one eye! You're a eye bigot! The whole world is a eye bigot!"

I did not ask the God of Glory and the Holy Road to forgive me for yelling that. I did not want forgiveness.

On our fourth day in Adabel, Oklahoma, Jackie got hired to wait tables at the Brown's Hotel coffee shop. It was a relief job, which meant evenings and a lot of weekends, but the deal included a pair of rubber-soled white shoes like nurses wear, two uniforms made out of shiny black material with white lacy stuff around the collar and the sleeves, and a cap thing to match.

Jackie said they hired her after giving her an audition. She had to take orders from a make-believe table of five where each one wanted a different kind of minute-steak sandwich with different kinds of things like mustard and catsup on it, with onions or without. Some wanted their onions raw, others fried. Some wanted french fries and others wanted chips or potato salad or slaw. Two ordered cherry cokes, one a large and the other a small. And there was a coffee, a milk and a chocolate malt. Well, she got it all straight going in and coming out and she said she chatted up and kidded the manager, hostess and head waitress like she had been doing it in Adabel, Oklahoma, all her life. She didn't say it, of course, but they surely all fell in love with her just like Pepper—and I—did.

On our fifth day I was hired by County Commissioner Sam Boone. I had tried two Skellys and a Texaco, a couple of grocery stores and the Rexall and the Western Auto, and nobody had work for a poor little one-eyed boy from Kansas. So I did what I never wanted to do again. I went to work spreading blacktop on roads. They told me at the courthouse

Commissioner Sam was looking for some help out at his road-crew barn north of town. I figured it was back to the roads and the blacktop or to nothing.

Commissioner Sam John Boone interviewed me in his office at the courthouse. He was as old as both of my grandfathers, wore a mustache like a lawyer and talked in a whisper like he was at a funeral. I could barely hear him. I had to tell him only two small lies. He asked me if I was a Democrat and if I had lived in Oklahoma all my life. I said, "Yes, sir," to both. I told him that my cousin sent off for Franklin Delano Roosevelt's autograph once and that I was from the town of Ida, which I knew from the Russell's guide game with Starch was about ninety miles southeast of here toward Texarkana. The one eye didn't bother him. But I figured it wouldn't.

"Spreading blacktop is work nobody around here much wants to do," he said. "Even the coloreds turn up their noses at it. And for them, getting covered with tar wouldn't even show."

He laughed and without thinking so did I.

Then I felt God-of-Glory-and-the-Holy-Road guilty afterward for doing so. Dad always said it was immoral to kid about a colored person's color and in Kansas nobody ever did. But this was Oklahoma.

Then I wondered about Ida, Oklahoma. Was there an Ida who was the wife, mother or daughter of the biggest man in town so they had to name the town after her?

Was that the deal on Adabel? Was there one daughter named Adabel or two daughters, one named Ada, the other Bel?

Hi, I'm Ada and this is my sister, Bel. We're a town called Adabel, Oklahoma.

175

Now that is some coincidence. I'm Ida and I'm a town all by myself ninety miles down the road toward Texarkana.

I asked Commissioner Sam for the story of how Adabel, Oklahoma, got its name. He whispered out a long story. It was about a surveyor for the Santa Fe Railroad named Davis Ardmore Denton who had a wife and a mother who hated one another. This spot was just an Indian trading post in a clump of trees with a couple of huts when he came through, picking the route of the Santa Fe coming down from Kansas City south to Texas. The railroad needed names for all the places along the route so he was told just to pick any he wanted. His wife's name was Ada so he named this place Ada. When he got to Dallas he sent a wire back to Chicago announcing to his wife that she was now the name of a place in Oklahoma. Western Union delivered it by mistake to the wrong Mrs. Davis Ardmore Denton, his mother, who was fit to be tied. When he got back to Chicago, his mother, whose name was Bel, threatened to take her own life and to tell his wife about an awful affair he had had with a red-headed tavern hustler in Galesburg, Illinois, when he first went with the railroad, if he didn't change the name.

The chief surveyor for Santa Fe said it was too late to make too big a change because Ada was already on a lot of the new maps. Maybe a little one could be made, he said.

" 'What about sticking "Bel" on the back end?' Davis Ardmore Denton asked," Commissioner Sam whispered. " 'Can we change it to Ada-Bel, Oklahoma?'

"The boss knew both Mrs. Dentons so he said, Fine. The mother did not take her own life, the wife never found out about the red-headed tavern hustler in Galesburg, and that's how Adabel, Oklahoma, got its name."

I saw it as just more proof of the strange way things sometimes work out.

Pepper was having his troubles finding Glory right away
in Adabel, Oklahoma. He had gone out looking for work
every morning every day the same way Jackie and I did. He
never came back with a job but he always had stories. Wonderful Tom Bell Pepper Bowen stories.

He went to Amberson's Ford and applied for a job as a
car salesman. The sales manager talked to him awhile and
then said, Let's take a spin in a new Galaxie and you drive.
Pepper didn't tell the man he didn't know how to drive a
car with a hydramatic automatic shift. He just got in behind
the wheel, put the lever in R instead of D and ran up over
a curb and crushed metal newspaper street-sales boxes from
the Adabel *Post-Times,* the Tulsa *World* and the *Daily Oklahoman* of Oklahoma City. One of the steel legs from the
Oklahoman box got stuck in the right front tire and blew it
out.

He went to Theodore Hamilton & Sons Lumber and Supply
and started coughing and sneezing the second he stepped in
some sawdust. He offended the owner of Continental Seed
and Feed by asking if he was hot with the top button on his
brown workshirt buttoned so tight there against his Adam's
apple. He told the lady at Russell Stover's that he didn't like
the taste of chocolate as much as he did root beer Life Savers.
He told the manager of Sooner Red Hardware that he was
just the second Catholic he had ever met and the first one
smelled like fish, particularly on Fridays, or was it just his
imagination?

I didn't know how many of the stories were true and didn't

even care. Jackie didn't either. It didn't matter at all except that all the stories added up to Pepper still not having a job.

His worst—or best—story was about what happened at the funeral home that had advertised for an experienced helper. The head funeral director asked Pepper where he had received his training and Pepper said at the Trailways School for Morticians in Leavenworth, Kansas.

"Trailways like in the bus company?" asked the man.

"No. Trailways as in End-of-the-Trail-ways," Pepper said.

The man asked Pepper to audition for him like the folks at Brown's coffee shop had asked Jackie to do. He took Pepper into a room where a guy about Pepper's age was shaving the face of a naked dead man with shaving cream and a Schick safety razor. The director asked Pepper to finish the shaving. Pepper said he was getting sicker by the moment as the other guy stood aside and handed him the Schick like it was the key to the First National Bank of Kansas City.

Pepper took the Schick in hand, leaned over the dead man and threw up on his naked chest.

Jackie and I didn't talk about it but I was sure she was thinking the same thing I was thinking at the end of our fifth day in Adabel, Oklahoma. What does Tom Bell Pepper Bowen usually do when he thinks he needs to acquire some money like everyone else?

He steals something.

I feel awful that I even had thoughts like that, considering what happened on our incredible sixth day in Adabel, Oklahoma.

I was about to leave for the courthouse around eight o'clock that morning. Commissioner Sam needed me to sign some papers so I could start to work. My first day would be in three days. Pepper was sitting on a flowered couch in the downstairs parlor by himself.

"Jackie had the early relief shift this morning," he said, like he was talking to a stranger on the bus from Topeka.

"We ought to go over there, have a cup or something and watch her in action," I said.

"Later," he said.

"Later than what?"

"Later than after we go to see Brother Walt at the First Church of the Holy Road."

" 'We' means only you, Brother Pepper."

"You became a Holy Road way back there in Lufkin. Remember?"

"It was the real-life nightmare of my life. 'Come to Glory, Brother. Come to Glory, Brother.' "

Pepper stood up and grabbed me by the arm. "It's time to come to Glory again, Brother Mack."

"Why?"

"I need a job."

"With the Holy Roads?"

"Amen, Brother Mack."

"No!"

"It's either that or . . . well . . ."

I had never been inside a church as big as the First Church of the Holy Road, Adabel, Oklahoma. It was larger than the Houston bus depot including the outdoor loading dock. The Lufkin courthouse and the Galveston Santa Fe station would have fit inside it. Only the Texas Capitol building in Austin was bigger.

The first thing we saw were two huge, I mean huge, portraits hanging there on the wall of the main entrance hallway.

One was of Brother Walt like on the welcome-to-Adabel billboard coming into town. The other was of Jesus Christ. They were the same size and they hung side by side. Like equals. Both were in color. Both were smiling. Both were in charge.

"Hi, guys," said Pepper to the portraits. "I'm Pepper. My friend here is called The One-Eyed Mack."

"Mack as in truck," I said.

"Pepper as in hot," he said.

We followed an arrow pointing up a flight of stairs to the "Pastor's Office." We went into the office and announced our arrival to a lady Holy Road sitting behind a desk. She reminded me a little bit of the woman who did the same kind of work for Governor Shivers. Only she wasn't sniffing and frowning like her, because Pepper didn't smell anymore.

"We are here to see Brother Walt," Pepper announced to the woman, who was a big grinner about thirty-five, with black hair running down her back.

"Well, that is so wonderful," she said. "Is it about the Lord's business?"

"Yes, ma'am," Pepper said. "We are here to follow Brother Walt down the Holy Road to Glory."

"Brother Walt is a follower himself," she said. "Jesus Christ our Lord is the leader."

"Amen," said The Pepper.

It wasn't but a few minutes later that we were in the presence of Brother Walt. He looked in person just like his wall and billboard portrait. I could see some artist coming to his house every morning and painting on his glasses and his nose and his ears and his hair and his eyebrows and his shirt and his tie and his suit.

He had a major-league manager's look to him. Or maybe

it was closer to an owner's. In other words, he may share the
wall with Jesus but it was clear he was the man really in
charge around here.

I liked the looks of him very much.

"God is Great," he said. He shook our hands and sat us
down in chairs and hit our backs and made us feel like we
were the two most important strangers he had ever met on
the Holy Road to Glory.

His voice was creamy and strong enough to do Cardinals
play-by-play on the radio or work the PA at the ball park.

It was clear Pepper liked him right off, too, and he got
right to it.

"I want to help you spread the word to the people of Adabel
about the Holy Road to Glory," he said. "I want to make it
my life's work from this day forward."

Brother Walt's blue eyes turned bright like little pencil
flashlights. "God is Great," he said. "Glory, Glory, Glory in
the highest. The angels are clapping. The saints are singing."

I didn't hear a thing but Brother Walt could probably have
convinced me I did.

"I wish to join your staff," Pepper said, moving right on
in like nothing I had ever seen before. I wondered whether
if I had used this technique on Junior Dillard and Mr. Starch
things would have worked out differently with The Thunderbird.

"Are you a two-man team?" Brother Walt asked, looking
right at me.

"He is my friend who is a Born-Again Holy Road and is
my only reference."

"Tom Bell Pepper Bowen is the kind of man we all need
with us on the Holy Road to Glory," I said like a reference
should.

Brother Walt took a deep breath, let it out slowly, squared his shoulders like he was about to dive into the Oklahoma Sooner line and got serious and down to business.

"Are you a graduate of one of our Holy Road seminaries?" he asked Pepper.

"No, sir, but I know . . ."

"Are you an ordained minister of the Gospel in our faith or any other faith?"

"Ordained only by God himself on the Holy Road," Pepper said.

It was not working. Brother Walt was not buying. He stood up.

"Come with me," he said. "Both of you."

He walked out of the office with strides that seemed to shake the building and the ground. He led us out down the stairs, outside to the sidewalk and then across the street and around the corner to the county courthouse.

"There is a young man I want you to meet," he said as Pepper and I trotted to keep up.

But that's all he said.

We followed him through a ground-floor door marked: SHERIFF'S OFFICE—JAIL.

Deputies and clerks and guards and prisoners all perked up when they saw Brother Walt. It wasn't quite like when Randolph Scott walked into a Marine barracks in the movies but it was almost. Nobody saluted but everybody nodded or smiled or trembled like they knew this man with the rosy cheeks and glasses and strong walk was important and tough.

In a few short minutes we were in a cell with a young man about my age. The cell was the size of the bathroom at the rooming house, only it was dirtier. The young man was also dirty and he smelled like Pepper did before love changed everything.

"Convert him," Brother Walt said to Pepper. "Make him see the Holy Road is the way to go, the only way to go. I have tried and I have tried. But I cannot. Do it and do it now and you have a job."

Pepper stepped forward and things started happening. Fast.

"Pepper!" yelled the young man in the cell. "Tom Bell Pepper Bowen in person!"

He grabbed Pepper by the hands and arms and started shaking everything he could. "It's me. Johnny. Johnny the Runt. You remember me from Fort Worth. We did a Piggly Wiggly burglary together...."

"There must be some mistake," Pepper said quickly.

But not quick enough.

The guard with the key had heard it all. And in a minute a tall chief deputy was there with a loose-leaf notebook of Wanted circulars.

And a minute after that Pepper was taken away in handcuffs.

"What is your name?" the tall chief deputy said to me.

I told him.

"He's The One-Eyed Mack and he's clean!" Pepper yelled as he was taken down the hall. "He's clean! Leave him alone!"

The chief deputy started looking in his Wanted book again.

"Don't tell Jackie, Mack!" was the last thing I heard Pepper yell.

Was the chief deputy going to find a bulletin sheet in his book that said:

WANTED. The One-Eyed Mack. For Burglarizing Bus Depot, Lufkin, Texas. For Theft of Russell's Official

183

National Motor Coach Guide. For Theft of Gertrude the Flexible. For Coming on the Beaumont Rocket. For Lying to Everyone He Meets. Description: Wears Black Eyepatch on Left Eye and Funny Hat on Head. Carries White Roebaugh-Buck's Bag.

The chief deputy was a slow reader and the book was thick so we stood there for a couple of lifetimes before he slammed it shut and said, "Nothing. He's all yours, Brother Walt."

"God is Great. What about the other one?"

"He's one of the Bad Bowens. There are scads of warrants out for him."

"Have his crimes been serious?"

"Yes, sir, they have."

"God is Great. Can we see him?"

"Yes, sir. Give me thirty minutes to get him processed and situated."

"Thank you. God is Great."

Brother Walt had come alive.

"There is no better way to start the day than with a sinner," he said to me. "A real sinner. A serious sinner."

He put an arm on my shoulder and we walked out of the jail, the sheriff's office and the courthouse like father and son, uncle and nephew, terminal manager and ticket agent.

"Serious sinners like your friend the Bad Bowen don't come along very often here in Adabel, Oklahoma. They are like meatloaf on Saturday night for those of us who have been called to lead the people down the Holy Road to Glory. This is a wonderful day. A wonderful day. Can I buy you a cup of coffee and a fresh powdered sugar–covered doughnut at Brown's coffee shop? What was your name again?"

"The One-Eyed Mack."

"Mack?"

"As in truck."

"God is Great."

13

Semper Fi

Brother Walt was treated like he was the king of Adabel, Oklahoma, when he walked into the Brown's Hotel coffee shop, just like he was at the county jail. Every customer and the waitresses and the cook and the cashier smiled and waved and grinned and nodded.

I went over and sat down at a table while he made what he called a Round of Joy to speak personally to and shake a hand or pat the back of everyone in the place. Jackie gave me one fabulous smile, like she didn't exactly know what was up but there I was with the man on the billboard. If he was the king of Adabel, then maybe I was the prince or the duke?

I had already decided not to tell her right away about Pepper. Pepper had said not to, for one thing. There was no point in worrying her until I had some more information, for another.

Did it mean Pepper was going on to prisons in three states and fourteen counties? Did it mean the plan to be lieutenant governor of Oklahoma was dead and done?

Brother Walt finished his Round of Joy and sat down at the table with me.

"Are you, too, a committer of serious crimes?" he asked in a voice loud enough to be heard in Leavenworth, Kansas, and other faraway places. "Is that what you and your Bad Bowen friend have in common?"

"No, sir," I whispered like Commissioner Sam, in hopes Brother Walt would take the hint and drop his voice, too. He didn't.

"You can tell me everything," he bellowed, like he was about to announce the singing of "The Star-Spangled Banner." "Committers of crimes and lesser sins are my tunafish sandwiches for lunch."

"Tunafish is my favorite sandwich," I said like I had laryngitis. "But I hate it with egg in it."

"God is Great!" he shouted. "Me too."

"I eat mine with a Grapette. How about you?"

"Milk. Always with a glass of cold, fresh sweet milk from Glencliff Dairy right here in town."

I wanted to say, "Milk is great but Grapette is greater," but what I really said was, "Sounds wonderful."

One of the other waitresses came and took our coffee and powdered sugar–covered doughnut orders. I was so happy Jackie's assigned area was way on the other side of the coffee shop.

I loved powdered sugar–covered doughnuts but they were hard to eat without getting the powdered sugar all over me. None of it got on Brother Walt. There he sat in a dark blue suit with a dark purple and red tie and a white shirt, and not a speck of powdered sugar dropped on anything. I didn't even see any around his mouth and lips.

Was it a miracle? Or did He fix it that way as a special deal for Holy Road preachers?

"The thirty minutes is nearly up," he said. "I can hardly wait to get back over to the jail to talk to your Bad Bowen friend."

"His name is Pepper. Tom Bell Pepper Bowen. His wife is named Jackie and she is the beautiful waitress over there on station on the other side near the hotel entrance. Both her and Pepper's daddies are in Leavenworth."

Brother Walt turned around and looked at Jackie and then back at me. When he said dealing with sinners was like meatloaf on Saturday night or a tuna sandwich for lunch he meant it. He was one very happy Holy Road preacher.

"Your daddy in Leavenworth, too?" he said like he really hoped so.

"No, sir. He's a Kansas State Highway Patrolman."

"Don't lie like that, young man, for no reason. Jesus will take away your smile." He rose from the table. "Let's go see the Bad Bowen."

Pepper looked whipped, gone, embarrassed. He still had his regular clothes and face and body but he was older and sick and different.

"Please, please tell me you have not told Jackie," he said the second Brother Walt and I stepped into his cell. It was down the hall but identically tiny, dirty and smelly to the one Johnny the Runt was in.

"I have not told Jackie."

"I knew this was going to happen eventually, Mack. It had to. I should never have married Jackie. I should have just turned myself in and gotten it all behind me. I should never

189

have brought her and you to Oklahoma, to this place. To think I had got to thinking I really could be lieutenant governor of Oklahoma someday. Think of that. A guy with a record a mile long and I let my crazy old man let me think I could . . ."

Brother Walt held up his right hand for silence. "God is Great and He is here," he said. "He will point the way out of this for you and you will follow that way. Is that clear, Mister Bad Bowen?"

"Come on now, Reverend, you can forget all of that mashed potato," Pepper said. "I lied to you about this Holy Road stuff. I do not know how to do anything except burglarize bus stations and hold up Safeways. I cheat people out of food and money and anything I decide I want. I walk against red lights and cross in the middle of the block. I throw up on dead men's chests and I lie. Oh, do I ever lie. I lie to my wife and I lie to my only friend, The One-Eyed Mack here. . . ."

"Hush, hush now."

"I am a Bad Bowen. Both my mother and my father are in the pen and that's where I belong and where I'm going. I am wanted in fourteen counties in three states. I am the plague. I am just the kind of person you and the Holy Roads need to burn at the stake, to stamp off the face of the earth."

"Shut up!"

Never had I heard or imagined hearing those two words delivered like Brother Walt delivered them. The bars in the cell window rattled. So did the brains and teeth in my head. Everybody in Adabel, Oklahoma, must have heard him. I wondered if everybody shut up until they figured out Brother Walt was talking only to this funny little Bowen guy in the county jail.

"On your knees!" he boomed at Pepper.

"I don't want to go on my knees," Pepper said. I was proud of his courage.

"On your knees, I said!" Then Brother Walt turned to me. "You, too, Mister One-Eye!"

I went down on my knees.

So did Pepper then.

Brother Walt put his left hand on Pepper's shoulder and bowed his head.

"Blessed Father in heaven, look at what we have here. We have a young man caught up in the chewing gum of crime and sin. A young man who looks down the Holy Road of life now and sees a fallen tree across the road. A young man who has awakened to find that his worst nightmares are now no longer nightmares. They are his life. A young man who will never again know the joy of tuna at lunch, meatloaf on Saturday night. A young man whose own sins have condemned him to a life behind four steel walls and a locked steel door. A young man who searched for Glory and found Hades.

"A young man who belongs to you, Blessed Father in Heaven."

"Forget all of this . . . stuff," Pepper said. I had never heard him say a really foul word but I felt one coming then.

Brother Walt the Billboard Man didn't pay any attention to Pepper. He had his eyes tightly closed, his head bowed slightly at an angle like he was listening to something.

"Jesus, our Lord and Savior, has spoken. You shall join the Marines and go to war instead of to prison."

He said it like he had just read it in the Bible. "You shall join the Marines and go to war instead of to prison—Ecclesiastes 6:14."

"What war?" I asked.

"The Korean War," Brother Walt answered.

"Never heard of it," Pepper said.

I hadn't either.

Brother Walt came with me to get Jackie after work at the coffee shop and asked her to come with us to his office at the First Church of the Holy Road.

"Pepper's dead, isn't he?" she said immediately.

"No, no, sweet daughter of God," said Brother Walt. "God is Great."

He sat her down on a couch in his office with me at her side. Then he pulled a chair right up in front of her and sat down. He leaned across and took her right hand in his.

"Sweet daughter of God..."

"My name is Mrs. Jackie Alice Bowen and I am not a Holy Road so please do not talk to me like I am one."

"My name is Reverend Walter Joe Jameson and I am a Holy Road."

"I know that. Everybody knows that. You put it up on a billboard."

"Do you know where your husband is now?"

"He's dead. I know he's dead. They always get preachers to tell wives when their husbands are dead."

She looked hard at me.

"Pepper is not dead, Jackie," I said.

"Then he's had both legs amputated, is that it?"

"No, no," Brother Walt said.

"His arms have been cut off?"

"No..."

"Then what happened? Why am I sitting here and why are you holding my hand? What is the bad news?"

"Your husband is in the county jail," Brother Walt said.

Jackie closed her eyes, bowed her head for a count of three or four and took a very deep breath. Then she looked back up and right at me. "He couldn't even be good for six days, could he, Mack? What did he do, rob a bank?"

"He didn't do anything new." I was a little annoyed that she would even think such a thing. "They got him on a bunch of piddling warrants from other places. We went over there to convert a prisoner to follow the Holy Road to Glory and he recognized Pepper."

"Can I go see him?" she asked.

"Jackie, there is something else going on about it," I said. I could feel my lip twitching like it always did every time I got up in class at school to say something.

"They're going to electrocute him, is that it?"

"No, Mrs. Bowen, that is not it," said Brother Walt. "He is going to join the U.S. Marines to keep from having to stay in jail."

She closed her eyes again and bowed her head and took a deep breath. This time when she brought her head back up and opened her eyes, they were full of tears.

"Isn't that worse than being electrocuted?"

Pepper left Adabel three Saturday afternoons later on The Thunderbird for Oklahoma City. There he would change to Greyhound and go on to a Marine base in San Diego, California, for boot camp or what the Marine recruiter from Tulsa, Sergeant Moyola, called "a very special vacation in sunny California." Jackie saw him off at Mr. Starch's bus depot. Brother Walt and I came too. So did Sergeant Moyola.

Staff Sergeant Bill D. Moyola was a Stan-the-Man kind of guy. I had never before seen a Marine in uniform, in person. The closest I came was Randy T. Whiteside, a Kansas State

Highway Patrolman who worked with Dad for a while out of McPherson. He had been a Marine in World War Two but I didn't know him then. He was six feet, three inches tall, had Charles Atlas muscles in his arms, neck and legs, and wore his hair in a quarter-inch GI. He was suntanned brown as a football, walked like he was the king of the Sorghum Festival and talked ever so politely in a MGM-movie-lion growl. I couldn't think of anything scarier than looking in the rearview mirror and watching Randy T. Whiteside get out of his patrol car and then come over to your car window and say, "Sorry to bother you, sir, but I just clocked you going twenty-seven miles per hour in a twenty-five-mile-an-hour zone. Would you please step out of your car so I can crush you to bits with my bare hands? Thank you."

Sergeant Moyola wasn't like that. He was short, thin, friendly and fun. He kept telling everybody not to shoot him because he was a Yankee Italian from Philadelphia. He knew more about baseball than anybody in the world and could rattle off the entire rosters of the Dodgers, Giants, Phillies and Cardinals like they were multiplication tables in school. He also knew Stan the Man's batting average and Harry the Cat's win-loss record for every year since they broke in. He said he started memorizing baseball statistics as something to do when he was a prisoner of the Japanese in the war.

Sergeant Moyola made me want to be a Marine, too. But that wasn't possible even to dream about. If the Kansas State Highway Patrol, Junior Dillard and Mr. Starch wouldn't take people with no left eyes, the U.S. Marines certainly wouldn't. I figured the Red Chinese would have to be marching down the middle aisle of the First Church of the Holy Road before anybody would hand me even a Daisy air rifle to defend Adabel, Oklahoma.

Brother Walt and Sergeant Moyola had worked hard with district attorneys and sheriffs in Kansas, Texas and Oklahoma to get all the charges dismissed against Pepper so he could enlist. Pepper had not murdered or raped or pointed a gun at anyone so it wasn't too hard to get it done. A district attorney in Comanche, Texas, where Pepper was wanted for writing a twenty-four-dollar hot check, was a problem. The check had been written to the district attorney himself for an old dark-brown dress suit and he wanted some personal justice. Sergeant Moyola got a Marine recruiter from San Antonio to drive up there one afternoon in full dress-blue uniform, and the district attorney finally saw his way clear to do his patriotic duty for the U.S. Marine Corps and America's fight to hold back the Chinese communists. Brother Walt had to get a Holy Road preacher in Chickasha, Oklahoma, to fall on his knees before a justice of the peace and claim Jesus Himself had personally recruited Tom Bell Pepper Bowen for the Marines to get a petty theft charge dismissed. Pepper had walked into a Rexall there and shoplifted a sack full of shoe polish, toothpaste and Milky Ways. The justice of the peace's sister owned the Rexall.

Pepper kept asking Brother Walt why it had to be the Marines. Why not just go into the Army or the Navy?

"Your record's too long," Brother Walt said once, twice, maybe three times. "Joining the Army or Navy would take care of only half of those charges against you. For a Bad Bowen only the Marines will do. They need volunteers right now."

None of us knew there was a Korean War going on. Why

people on buses like the Map Man, Lillian the Come Lady and others like Governor Allen Shivers and Mr. Starch didn't mention it, I'll never know. America being in a war and all of us Americans not knowing about it was really not too terrific. But it wasn't all our fault. Shouldn't the President of the United States send people around to bus stations or do whatever else it takes to make sure good Americans like Pepper, Jackie and me knew there was a war going on in a place called Korea? What was the hurry to have another war so soon after World War Two anyhow? They were going to have to make a whole new bunch of war movies, for one thing.

Sergeant Moyola sat me down on a bench outside on the courthouse lawn to explain it to me. It didn't take long. He said some Koreans who were communists invaded the southern part of Korea where the Koreans weren't communists. The Chinese were helping those in the north and we had come to help those in the south. President Truman, who was from Missouri, made the decision.

There was a statue of a World War One soldier on the courthouse lawn that reminded me a lot of the one in Lufkin. A new, fresh, empty stone platform for a World War Two soldier was next to it. The sergeant said the statue was on its way to Adabel now, on a truck from Raleigh, North Carolina, where a famous sculptor man had made the statue. He said the sculptor used a young Adabel soldier who was really killed in the war as the model.

He did it from his high school annual and other photographs from family and friends.

Jackie stood right there with Pepper at the bus door through all the good-byes.

Brother Walt shook Pepper's right hand like he was pumping for well water and said "God is Great" eight or nine times and promised to put him in his daily prayers and his Sunday-morning prayers and his Wednesday-night prayers.

Sergeant Moyola said the Marine Corps motto was *"Semper Fidelis,"* which meant "Always Faithful." He said Marines said "Semper Fi" to each other a lot like a password. He told Pepper it was only one of many traditions he would learn as he wore the uniform of the proudest and best. "Semper Fi, Pepper," he said, and saluted him.

Then it was my turn. I had memorized the words Stan the Man said to the batboy as he went to the plate in the sixth game of the 1946 World Series. "I'll go up there and take the best cut I can and when it's over, win or lose, I will know I did my best even if I strike out or pop it to short."

None of that would come out so I just said what I felt. "You're the only buddy I have. So be careful." Then I looked at the bus. "It's a Flxible like Gertrude. That means good luck."

"Yeah," Pepper said. "I don't have another buddy like you either."

"Good."

"Good?"

"Don't ask me any more questions. Be a good Semper Fi Marine and come back and be the lieutenant governor of Oklahoma."

"Sergeant Moyola says I had better get used to calling everybody sir like you do. So I say to you, Yes, sir, Mister One-Eyed Mack, sir.'"

We shook hands and I walked back into the bus depot to wait for Jackie.

Brother Walt and Sergeant Moyola said they would leave

it to me to walk Jackie back home if I thought that would be all right. I said, "Yes, sir," to both.

"You'd have been a great Marine, Mack," Sergeant Moyola said. And he said it like he meant it.

I did not look back outside to the loading dock and to the bus until I heard the motor revving and the air brakes swishing.

Jackie stood right there and waved and kept waving at the back of that bus, at the upside-down-comma back of that bus until it was way, way out of sight, until it was halfway to Oklahoma City.

She was so gorgeous she could have done it in a movie. She was dressed in a blue dress with short sleeves and dark blue stripes around the collar. It was her best dress. Her short hair was perfectly clean and combed as usual. She had a little rouge on her cheeks and some good red lipstick on her lips.

We didn't say a word to each other for a block after we left the bus depot. She had been crying but now that was over.

"I'm going to have a baby, Mack," she said just as we turned the corner at Broadway and Main by the courthouse and started up those last three blocks to her apartment house.

I don't remember what I said first. I remember stumbling over my feet and grabbing her left hand tightly.

"I just found out for sure yesterday," she said.

"What a going-away present for Pepper," I said. "Wowee. He must have been so excited."

"I didn't tell him, Mack." She was still walking at a steady pace.

"Why not, for goodness sake?" I squeezed her hand even tighter as if that would help her answer me.

"Going off to be a Marine to keep from going to prison in three states and fourteen counties was enough for him to handle at one time. Going to be a daddy, too, would be too much. I'll write him a long letter about it."

"Daddy?" I said before I thought. "It's hard to see Pepper as a daddy."

"He'll be a wonderful daddy, Mack."

"Yes, ma'am."

14
Roy and Them

I got my first letter from Pepper three weeks and two days after he left on that Thunderbird Flxible for Oklahoma City. It was on regular stationery that was white with a small brown Marine emblem up at the top. I had never seen Pepper's penmanship before. It was slanted way too much to the right and was shaky and big like a little boy's. But I could read it.

Dear Mack:

Don't show this letter to Jackie or tell her anything that's in it. I want her to think being a Marine is just fine like Sergeant Moyola said and I am just fine. She'd worry about me if she knew the truth. I know the truth and I worry about me.

It's awful, Mack. I do not know how Randolph Scott and John Payne and Tyrone Power and all of them stood it. The first thing they did was shave my head. I mean they sat me down in a chair and a guy with a giggle ran one of those electric barber tools back and forth across the top of my head four or five times and that was it. Next! Some doctor made me take all my clothes off and cough. He asked me if I liked girls. They make me run up and down stairs with a trash can over my head. They get us up at 5 in the morning and make us run around a parade field and jump up and down like monkeys. Sergeants they call D.I.'s come through all the time sticking their fingers into our rifles and our lockers and everywhere else to see if there is dust or dirt. They yell at us like they hate us. They use language that I believe Brother Walt would say is so bad any user of it would be beyond even his reform. I didn't cuss before I came here. But now I do. All the time. Marines talk worse than any people on the face of the earth. I've decided they're training us to cuss the Chinese Commies to death.

Tell Brother Walt going to jail in three states and fourteen counties would be meat loaf on Saturday night compared to this. No, don't say that. It's not true. Barely.

Your only buddy,
Pepper

His second letter came the very next day. It was shorter and was written on the back of a lined stationery sheet that had a colored picture of World War Two Marines putting a flag in the ground.

Dear Mack,

Yesterday they sent home a guy for wetting his bed. He was my age from Eugene, Oregon. The first time he did it the D.I. made him sleep in his wet bed that night. But he did it again so the D.I. made him wear the wet sheet over his uniform all day. A guy from Macon, Missouri, is in the bed next to me—Marines call beds Racks. Everything here has a different name than normal. ———— thinks the other guy wet his Rack on purpose so he could get out of the Marines and not have to go to Korea and fight the commies. I asked the guy if he was thinking about doing the same thing and he said, Maybe. He asked me if I was and I said, Maybe. Would I have to go to prison in three states and 14 counties if the Marines kicked me out for wetting the Rack?

I think if I just refused to cuss they would think that was even stranger than wetting the Rack and would send me home faster. I hate it here, Mack. I hate every single solitary thing about it.

Your only buddy,
Pepper

Brother Walt helped Jackie find a nice first-floor apartment in a big house not far from the hotel coffee shop. The apartment had two bedrooms, a kitchen and, most important, a bathroom that was all hers and only hers. The house was owned by one of his Holy Road widows who was easily persuaded to make room for a pregnant young woman whose husband was away in the Marines by kicking out a house painter and his wife who had just moved to town from Midlothian, Texas.

I stayed with my room on the third floor of the rooming house and with using the Skelly station men's room when necessary. I had gotten used to the life and moving again seemed like too much trouble right then. I always made a point to go by the coffee shop or the apartment to look in on Jackie and say hi. It was the most important thing I did every day.

Working for Commissioner Sam went great almost from the start, thanks again to Brother Walt. They only kept me on the blacktop crew for two weeks because of him. I ran into him on a street corner one evening on the way home from a day of spreading tar on the Stratford road—and all over me and my clothes.

"Nobody should be that dirty and black after a day's hard labor," Brother Walt said to me.

Two days later I almost fell on my knees right there in the road equipment barn and screamed Praise God and Glory in the Highest for Brother Walt when the foreman told me I was being switched to grading.

"You must be a real Holy Road to have that kind of pull with Brother Walt," he said. "Commissioner Sam can't afford to lose the Holy Road vote so whatever Brother Walt wants he gets. So there you are."

The foreman's name was Winchester and he said "So there you are" at the end of everything he said. Good morning, Mack, so there you are. How are the tires on Grader Five, so there you are?

I did not tell him I had pull with Brother Walt because of Tom Bell Pepper Bowen, one of the Bad Bowens. I did not tell him the best way to get on the best side of a preacher was to be the only buddy of a serious crook.

What if Jimmy T. had kicked that can just an inch or two the other way? What if I had caught the Texas Chief streamliner a day earlier or a day later? What if I hadn't decided to hop on The Beaumont Rocket?

Now there came another huge What If into my life. What

if Roy Rogers had not come to Adabel, Oklahoma, to make a movie?

He did come for two and one-half weeks. And he brought Dale Evans, Gabby Hayes and Trigger with him. For two and one-half weeks I woke up in my bed in that rooming house in Adabel, Oklahoma, and knew that Roy, Dale, Gabby and Trigger were also waking up in Adabel, Oklahoma. What the Camp Brady Bruce counselor had told me about Roy had not changed my opinion of Roy. I was one of his radio friends he called Buckaroos. And always would be. Marines said "Semper Fi" to one another. Buckaroos said "Happy Trails."

The movie they were making in Adabel was called *Oklahoma Critter*. It was about an incredibly smart and beautiful white palomino horse played by Trigger that nobody paid any attention to because it was "just an Oklahoma critter." Then along came a singing cowboy down on his luck played by Roy. He and his loyal, funny sidekick played by Gabby saw the horse and it was magic at first sight. They talked the owner, a dumb rancher played by a guy who always played dumb ranchers in Roy's movies, into letting them have the horse for "a song." But the rancher's daughter, a beautiful lady played by Dale, cried when her father let the horse go. "He may be just an Oklahoma critter," she said, "but I love him." But the father let Roy and Gabby take the horse anyhow "for the horse's good." Roy and Gabby taught the horse to do fabulous tricks and before long the three of them were going around Oklahoma, Texas and the rest of the world performing at rodeos, circuses and on the radio. Then one fateful, dramatic day at Madison Square Garden in New York City the horse refused to do any more tricks or to perform at all. He lay down and would not get up. A veterinarian examined him but could find nothing physically wrong. "If it was a human instead of a horse I'd diagnose his trouble as homesickness," said the vet, who was played by a guy who usually played deputy U.S. marshals. Roy thought and worried and finally packed up Trigger and Gabby and went off to Oklahoma. Sure enough, the horse got well and smart and beautiful again the minute he laid eyes on Dale and that Oklahoma ranch. Dale broke into song. Roy joined in. Then so did Gabby and the father. The movie ended with the Oklahoma Critter running and playing in an open Oklahoma field.

Roy, Dale, Gabby and the other actors were all staying at the John J. Wilson Circle W Ranch twenty-two miles southwest of town. Roy and Dale were known to be partial to Oklahoma because it was on another ranch in Oklahoma that they had been married by a preacher friend who came down from Oklahoma City.

They were busy making the movie so they didn't come into town that much. Whenever they did, the word spread like fire. Jackie saw Dale four times on the street or in a car, Roy twice and Gabby five or six times.

My experiences were much more special than that. First, I had a conversation with Gabby Hayes.

"Hi, there, son," he said to me at the Rexall where I had accidentally and luckily gone to buy some Colgate-Palmolive toothpaste. Gabby came in unannounced just like a normal person would and bought a pack of Luckies.

"Hi, Mister Hayes," I answered.

"Gabby's the name."

"Gabby. Yes, sir."

"Don't take any Okie nickels," he said, and he left.

Second. The Wilson ranch was on the state highway to Atoka but I was able to drive by there a few times on the way to grade various county roads. Once I saw Trigger in the pasture grazing by himself just like a normal horse. Another time a guy I didn't recognize was riding him, and the third time I saw him Roy Rogers himself was in the saddle. I waved but Roy must not have seen me because he didn't wave back.

Third came a What If thing that changed my life.

It happened the night before they all left Adabel for good. Roy invited the citizens of Adabel to come to the Orpheum Theater for a free night's thank-you entertainment.

A huge mob showed up, of course. Everybody in Adabel wanted to be thanked by Roy and Dale, Gabby and Trigger. Jackie and I got there two hours early but there was already a line that wound outside and around the block twice. Once it started moving it became sadly clear that we were not going to make it inside. There were too many people ahead of us.

But once again Brother Walt came along to deliver us. He saw us there in the line and asked us politely to come with him. He took us right up to the door in front of everybody like we were important people. The theater folks, afraid probably that he would bring the Holy Road God down on them if they didn't, smiled at Brother Walt and immediately found Jackie and me seats down in front on the second row right on the aisle.

I decided then that Brother Walt was probably the Second Son of God. The Bible said there would be a Second Coming but God decided to throw everybody off by sending his Second Son, Walt, instead of Jesus, the other son who already had had the first shot.

"Why is Brother Walt so nice to us?" Jackie asked as we sat down.

"He likes sinners," I said.

"I'm no sinner."

"You're kin to a few."

"That's not the same."

"Yes, ma'am."

Roy, Dale, Gabby and Trigger came out on the stage.

"Hi, Buckaroos," Roy said into the microphone in that chocolate ice cream voice of his.

"Hi, Roy!" Everyone of us in the Orpheum Theater yelled back as loud as we could.

"Hello there, Adabel, Oklahoma!" Dale yelled in her voice that always reminded me of a grilled cheese sandwich. Don't ask me why.

"Hi, Dale!" we shouted back.

"Hi, podners!" my friend Gabby yelled.

"Hi, Gabby!"

Trigger kind of pranced around and neighed once or twice.

"Hi, Trigger!" we all shouted.

Then Roy strummed his guitar and sang the first few lines of "Tumblin' Tumbleweeds."

Dale joined him for the final line or two and then she sang the next song by herself. It was "Love Is a State of the Heart in a State Called Texas." Roy sang a couple more and finally Gabby told some jokes.

"You know why cowboys smell so bad?" he asked us.

"No!" we shouted.

"Because they can't tell the difference between cow manure and Dorothy La-mure."

We all laughed and he asked: "What did the Oklahoman say to the guy from Idaho?"

He waited a few seconds to establish the fact that we did not know and he said, "He said, 'I'd rather be a Sooner than a Tater.'"

Gabby told a couple or so more like that and Roy and Dale sang a few more songs. Everybody loved every word, every note. It was so nice of them to do this for us and we all appreciated it very much.

I started wondering what they would do if Trigger decided to relieve himself right there on the Orpheum stage in front of Jackie, me and all of Adabel, Oklahoma. I didn't think it was possible to train horses to not do that kind of thing at certain times because I remember seeing horses do it in front of big crowds at the Cole Brothers Circus at Newton and at the Ringling Brothers in Wichita. Of course, Trigger was a special kind of movie horse. Maybe they have to be able to hold it in order to be in the movies.

Hi, what do you do for a living?

I train horses to hold it in public.

Are the hours good?

No, but I meet a lot of interesting horses.

Then as the show was winding up, the What If happened.

Roy Rogers, King of the Cowboys, said into the microphone: "We need a volunteer up here on the stage to help us say good-bye and thanks to all of you fabulous people of Adabel, Oklahoma, who have made our stay here so fabulous."

Several hands were raised but before I knew it Roy was pointing down and right at me. "You there, young man. You with the eyepatch. Come on up here." I hadn't even raised my hand. Or least, I don't think I did. It's possible I did without thinking.

I looked at Jackie. She was smiling like she was saying, Go ahead. So go ahead I did.

I kind of trotted down to one end of the stage and up the steps. And there I was, like magic, under the bright lights of the Orpheum Theater, Adabel, Oklahoma, and the world, with Roy Rogers, Dale Evans, Gabby Hayes and Trigger.

"What's your name?" Roy said once he got me over to the microphone.

"The One-Eyed Mack."

Roy laughed and so did everybody else except Trigger. I had never spoken into a microphone or heard my voice like that through a public address system. I sounded like Randolph Scott.

"Mack?" said Roy.

"Mack as in truck."

Roy bent over with laughter like he had a stomachache. The rest of the house came down, too, with laughs and claps. They loved me.

"What do you do here in Adabel, Oklahoma?" Roy asked me.

"I used to spread black tar on county roads and all over my hands, face and clothes. Now I just grade the roads with a grader."

Gabby came over and slapped me on the back. Dale gave me a peck on the cheek. Only Trigger remained calm.

"Well, well, well," said Roy, smiling and obviously liking me very much. "Dale and I are going to sing a song about you, One-Eyed Mack, and our other friends here in Adabel, Oklahoma."

He strummed his guitar a few times. Thinking, obviously. Composing, obviously. Then he stepped right up to the microphone and sang to the tune of "Home on the Range."

> "Oh, give me a home
> Where The One-Eyed Mack roams,
> Where the Buckaroos of Adabel play,

Where seldom we go,
Which is sad, sad to know,
'Cause we loved it here all through these days.

"Home, Home on this Range,
Where the Buckaroos of Adabel play,
Where The One-Eyed Mack spreads
Black tar all through these parts,
And Dale, Gab, Trigger and I
Lost our hearts."

Roy Rogers made up a song with my name in it! My name was sung from the stage of the Orpheum Theater by Roy Rogers, King of the Cowboys!

Then he sang it again:

"Oh give me a home
Where The One-Eyed Mack roams,
Where the Buckaroos of Adabel play,
Where seldom we go,
Which is sad, sad to know,
'Cause we loved it here all through these days."

"Everybody now," said Roy Rogers, King of the Cowboys. And we all sang:

"Home, Home on the Range,
Where the Buckaroos of Adabel play,
Where seldom we go,
Which is sad, sad to know,
'Cause we loved it here all through these days."

"Good-bye and God bless you all, Buckaroos," said Roy.

The show was over. The curtain went down. Roy shook my hand. Dale gave me another kiss. Two kisses on the cheek from Dale Evans! Two! That's one and then another. Two! Gabby shook my hand and slapped me on the back. "You're a natural for the stage and there's one leaving for Tulsa in fifteen minutes," he said, and laughed. So did I.

"How'd you lose the eye?"

"I didn't like what it saw one day so I just pulled it out and gave it a toss."

He guffawed like it was the funniest thing he had ever heard.

I looked over at Trigger, who was now being handled by a couple of hands from the Circle W Ranch. He had held it through the performance. Good work, Trigger. Proud of you, boy.

I went back out front and down the stage steps. I saw Mr. Starch from the bus depot. He gave me a kind of half-wave. Most of the rest of the people were already out of the theater. Jackie was still there waiting for me.

"Mack, you are wonderful!" she said, and I must admit I agreed with her.

We started walking up the aisle and there came Brother Walt, the Second Son of God.

"Mister One-Eyed Mack," he said, throwing an arm around my shoulder. "You have a natural talent for performance. God is Great."

"Thank you, sir."

"Don't thank me. Thank God. He gave to you the talent."

"Yes, sir."

"Have you ever thought of politics or preaching for a life's work?"

"No, sir."

"God is Great."

I decided not to tell him right then that I had begun to suspect that God was his daddy.

I wrote to Pepper that night about what had happened. I even told him about wondering how they knew Trigger wasn't going to mess up that Orpheum Theater stage in the middle of everything. I couldn't have said that to another soul. That's the kind of thing you can say only to a friend.

I had gotten a letter from him the morning before. It was a spooky letter. I usually just made up things to Jackie about what he said. She told me some of the things he said in her letters. Maybe she made up her versions, too.

The letter was written on a folded yellow card with a red Marine Corps flag on the top side.

Dear Mack,

I have been assigned to the First Marine Division. We are maybe leaving for Korea soon but I don't know when. They usually give leave before you go but not us. The D.I., who's turning out not to be as bad as I thought, said they needed more Marines over there in a hurry. That doesn't sound too hot because it probably means a lot of Marines are dying and they need more to kill. But don't tell Jackie. I am writing her that I am going to be a truck driver behind the lines somewhere. The truth is they have given me what is called a Browning Automatic Rifle. We Marines call them B.A.R.'s for short. They're a kind of machine gun and they weigh a ton. Everybody in the platoon says the B.A.R.'s are the first ones the Chinese go for. "Kill the B.A.R.!" is what they yell in

Chinese. They say you can hear them yell it all the way from Korea back to China. Kill the B.A.R.! Kill the B.A.R.! Listen carefully there in Adabel, Mack. You might be able to hear them, too. If you do, remember it's Tom Bell Pepper Bowen they're yelling about.

Your only buddy,
Pepper

P.S.—The next day. Didn't get it mailed last night because we went on a night hike through the rain to see if we would float or melt. The baby! How about me as a daddy? I just got Jackie's letter. Help me make sure my kid never finds out about my life before and about Mom and Dad and the family. Tell him (her?) that I was born a Marine with a B.A.R. in my hand.

If something should happen to me, Mack, I'll be depending on you to make sure Jackie takes care of herself and the baby. You're all there is for them really except for me.

I never in my whole life spent one split second thinking about being a daddy. Don't tell Jackie that.

I still can't believe it.

P.

15
Official Use Only

I was out in the heavy equipment yard trying to put a new generator belt on a Caterpillar road grader when a woman in the office paged me on the public address system. She said I was wanted in the office immediately. Immediately? We never did anything at Commissioner Sam's immediately except pave the driveways of his friends and relatives and contribute to the Reelect Commissioner Sam campaign fund.

I came outside and the first thing I saw was the Ford Fairlane sedan. It was dark olive green like the Marines' cars. Sergeant Moyola drove one. As I got closer I saw that's what it was. U.S. MARINE CORPS—OFFICIAL USE ONLY was painted on the car's front door in small yellow letters. A Marine was sitting in the front seat behind the wheel.

Official Use Only.

By the time I stepped inside the office and saw Sergeant Moyola and Brother Walt I knew what it was about. I knew exactly what was going on.

They waited until we were in the car. Sergeant Moyola did the talking.

"He was on a patrol with his squad. There was contact with the enemy. . . ."

What's "contact" mean?

" . . . Some chink threw a hand grenade down in the middle of them. . . ."

Was it like a tin can with a ragged lid?

" . . . Pepper saw it first, yelled for the others to take cover. . . ."

Take cover where?

" . . . He fell on it. . . ."

Did he hurt himself?

" . . . It exploded, of course. . . ."

Of course.

" . . . He died a hero, Mack. A first-class hero . . ."

Name all the classes of hero and you get an A on your report card.

" . . . They'll be giving him a high medal for valor, I'm sure. . . ."

Is valor like meatloaf on Saturday night?

" . . . We wanted you to be with us when we told Jackie. . . ."

She's going to have a baby!

" . . . This will be hard on her. . . ."

She's going to have a baby!

Brother Walt now spoke for the first time. He was sitting in the backseat next to me. Sergeant Moyola was in front with the other Marine. They told me he was a captain.

"She told me he was driving trucks way behind the lines," said Brother Walt. "Did you know differently?"

"God ain't so Great after all, is he?" I said.

"Birth comes first and death comes third. Life is second

and is what happens in between. There is no life in between without birth and death."

"Like tunafish salad between two pieces of bread?"

"Maybe."

"Who ever cared about Korea anyhow?"

"God cares."

"Who's in charge of caring about Jackie and her baby when it's born?"

"God has assigned that task of love to you and to me and to Sergeant Moyola and we are going to perform it with all the power and glory that are in our hearts and souls."

"Pepper was my only buddy."

"God will provide another."

"Like hell he will."

"God'll also take soap to that mouth of yours."

"For saying 'hell'?"

"God is Great."

"No he isn't."

I was crying like a baby now. Brother Walt put an arm around my shoulders and I put my head down on his shoulder.

Nobody said anything else until we drove up in front of the Brown's Hotel coffee shop.

I took a few minutes to get the wet and the red out of my eyes and then I went in to get her. The others stayed in the car so as not to startle and scare her.

"I need to see you outside for a minute, if I could?" I said to her as normally as humanly possible.

"Not right now, Mack," she said. She frowned at me, something she never did because I never gave her cause to. "Can't you see? We're awful busy right now."

I saw that, yes, they were awful busy right now. A couple of people I had never seen before in my life even gave me a wave. They knew me from my stint with Roy and them at the Orpheum Theater.

I stepped back and walked around to Maggie Winship, the woman in charge of the coffee shop. I told her an urgent emergency had come up involving Pepper, and I needed to take Jackie away to the church so she could be told about it.

"Is he dead?" Maggie said in a voice that was too loud. But Jackie was waiting on the bankers' table on the other side of the place. She hadn't heard.

I shrugged to Maggie like I was saying it was anybody's guess, and she said, "I'll go tell her it's all right to leave."

In a few seconds there Jackie was in front of me, frowning. "This had better be important, Mack. The place is full and getting fuller. It's afternoon coffee-break time. . . ."

We were out on the street before she knew it. She spotted the Marine Corps car. Sergeant Moyola got out. Uncle Walt got out.

"No! God, no!" She screamed. Her face was suddenly like snow and then like fire and then like wadded-up cellophane paper.

Brother Walt moved quickly toward her.

"I don't want to hear it," she said. "Don't tell me anything. No!"

Jackie turned and started running. I took out after her. So did Brother Walt and Sergeant Moyola. She was fast even in her waitress shoes and uniform.

I caught her at Okmulgee Avenue after just a half-block.

She resisted a second and then gave in, scrooched up like she wanted to get tinier so she could climb inside me and hide. I held her tight like I did Meg the night Momma died.

Jackie smelled like the perfume Pepper had given her in Leavenworth as a wedding present. "You already smell like perfume," he told her. "Use this for emergencies and special occasions." The best I could tell, every day since had been either an emergency or a special occasion because she always smelled like that perfume. It was called Sweet Blossom and that's what she was.

The Marine captain drove up with the car. We helped her inside and took her over to the church parsonage.

Brother Walt held her close to him during the ride. Nobody talked. Jackie just cried and sobbed and blew her nose.

But in the parlor of the parsonage somebody had to talk. The captain particularly had to talk so it could be official.

I decided this captain had the worst job in the world. What could be worse than going around to people and telling them officially that their son or husband or brother had just died in a war.

"You are Mrs. Jackie Alice Bowen, wife of Tom Bell Bowen, Private, U.S. Marine Corps. I am sorry to inform you that your husband was killed in action while serving his country against enemy forces in Korea...."

"Shut up!" Jackie screamed at him. "Shut up about Korea!"

"Well ... yes, ma'am."

He waited a full minute of silence before going on.

"You should know that Private Bowen has been recommended for a decoration for his heroism."

"I don't even know where Korea is!"

"I've been there. It's a beautiful country...."

"Shut up about Korea!"

The captain pulled an official-looking piece of paper out

of a briefcase and set it on the coffee table in front of her on the couch. He looked at Sergeant Moyola and they both stood up.

"I know it doesn't help even a tiny bit right now, Mrs. Bowen," the captain said, "but your husband died a hero. There should be bridges or schools or highways named for him and songs written about him and monuments built to him.

"He gave his life so others might live, Mrs. Bowen."

The two Marines left the room.

It was very late that night when I got back to my rooming house. There in the sitting room was my dad reading the Adabel *Post-Times.* He was in the same chair Pepper was in that sixth-day morning he told me he was going to go see Brother Walt about joining him on the Holy Road to Glory.

Dad was in his dark blue civilian suit, the one he had on in Houston and wore to funerals and other church events.

"Hello, son." He stood and stuck his right hand out to me. "It's been a while since you jumped train in Hillsboro, Texas."

"Yes, sir." I took his hand but only for a quick second. Shaking his hand was like putting your hand under a truck.

"The lady here gave me this paper to read about what happened to you and Roy Rogers. It must have been some night."

"Best night ever."

"Sorry I missed it."

I went over and sat down in a chair off to one side from his. He sat back down.

"How's Meg?"

"Fine. Just fine, son. She sends her love."

"I love her, too."

"She wants to know if you are ever coming home."

"Tell her for visits, yes, sir."

"Just for visits?"

"Yes, sir."

"Is that final for life?"

"Nothing's final for life except when you die."

"When's your first visit?"

"It won't be long."

"The paper says you're working on roads again?"

"That's the only job God allows for one-eyed people."

"I talked to Junior Dillard at The Thunderbird the other day. He said he's got an opening for a ticket agent and thinks you'd be fine for it. You remember him?"

"Did you have to hold a pistol to his head to get him to say that?"

"No, son. He brought it up naturally on his own."

I stood up. "Tell him it's too late now. I needed that job way back in my other life. Not this new one."

Dad was on his feet now. He didn't want to be, but he had to. "Then that's it for now?"

"Yes, sir."

We shook hands again but I did not look him in the eye. He walked to the door and I started up the steps to my room on the third floor.

"Would you come home, son, if your mother was alive and there at the house?"

God, what a question. What a lousy, awful, rotten, unfair, stupid, dumb, ridiculous question. Doesn't he know dead people do not come back from the dead to see their sons or their only buddies?

"You ever had a friend die who you would have given your toe to if he asked for it?" I said to Trooper Dad.

But he was already out the front door and I was on the second-floor landing on my way to the third by the time I said it.

There were questions about Pepper's next of kin. I told Sergeant Moyola about Pepper's mom and dad being in prison. I felt I had to. They'll be easy for the government to notify, he said. Brother Walt got Commissioner Sam to call the congressman who represented Adabel to see if some strings could be pulled to get both his mom and his dad out of prison on special passes to attend their son's funeral.

I was there in Brother Walt's office when Commissioner Sam whispered the results of his efforts.

"He said he checked with the Bureau of Prisons and it was out of every possible question," he said. "The President of the United States would have trouble getting that done. They've both got records ten miles long."

"All the more reason they should be here for the burial of their son, an American hero," said Brother Walt, lover of all people with criminal records. The longer the better.

"The congressman also asked that none of us tell anyone of his efforts on this matter," said Commissioner Sam. "For obvious reasons."

"Those reasons are not so obvious to me, Sam," Brother Walt said.

"It would not be good for the image of Adabel or for this county or this congressional district if it was known we were burying a boy at Oak Lawn Cemetery who has a father at Leavenworth and a mother at the Federal Prison for Women at Alderson, West Virginia."

"He jumped on a hand grenade, Sam. The boy gave his life so others may live. He was a United States Marine."

"But he really wasn't from here, you know."

"God is Great." Brother Walt stood up and looked over at me. "Shall we pray, Mack?"

"Yes, sir," I said, as I always said when Brother Walt said "Shall we pray?"

Brother Walt closed his eyes and held his right hand high above his head, palm forward.

"Dear Father in Heaven, forgive Sam for he clearly knows not what he says and does. He clearly knows not that it is a sin against the Word not to honor the martyr, the hero, the dead sons of our beloved country, the fallen men of the United States Marine Corps. Forgive him if you can, dear Father. Amen."

I opened my eyes and saw Commissioner Sam's normally weathered brown face was near white.

"Walt," he whispered in a sweat. "I meant nothing like that. Nothing."

"Pray on your knees tonight, Sam. Maybe it will pass."

"Sure. You bet."

Commissioner Sam backed toward the door like the Holy Ghost was coming at him with a Louisville Slugger.

It was a Tuesday afternoon and by all rights I should have probably gone back to the road barn and my job. Brother Walt took care of that.

"I will be needing Mack here to help me the rest of the day doing the work of the Lord," he said. "Is that a problem for you, Sam?"

"No problem. No problem at all."

After he was gone, Brother Walt said only: "With God's help we should be able to do better than that."

"Better than what that?"

"Better than that as county commissioner."

*　　*　　*

Thirty minutes later I was out on Waurika Avenue on the way to the laundry when I saw Dad again. I had assumed he had gone back to Kansas. But there was that walk again. It was either him or Alan Ladd or Marshall M. Mooney, the Map Man.

It was Marshall M. Mooney, the Map Man.

Who's next? Will Lillian the Come Lady and Governor Shivers and the no-tongue short-order cook and the plumber and everyone else from my New Life now drop in on me at Adabel, Oklahoma?

Mr. Mooney had his head down, of course, and was coming right toward me on the sidewalk.

"Hey there, mister," I said when he got to me. "Do you happen to know where I could get my hands on a good map of Arkansas?"

He stopped, looked up, smiled and looked down again so quick it could have been one move.

"Help me, Mack," he said. "I'm looking for a man they call The Cat. That's all I know. He's from Adabel, Oklahoma, and they call him The Cat."

"Harry the Cat Brecheen?"

"Maybe. Yes, maybe."

"He's one of the finest left-handers in the National League. Won three games in the forty-six World Series."

"Gertrude met him in St. Louis."

"The Cat pitches for the St. Louis Cardinals."

"Must be him. Yes. We must hurry. I must get back on the bus as soon as possible. There's still so much to do."

"It's baseball season. He's off playing somewhere."

"Help me, Mack. I must get back on the bus before the storm comes."

It was one of those Oklahoma afternoons I was learning to know that made you feel like God was hovering right over town trying to decide whether to flood the place out with rain, beat it to a pulp with hail or just pick it up and spread it around a bit with a tornado. The clouds were dark gray and were racing each other across the dark, dark blue sky. There was no telling what was going to happen eventually. Sometimes nothing did.

Nothing had by the time Mr. Mooney and I got to the Brecheen house on Fourth Street.

"Sorry to bother you," I said to a nice woman who came to the door. "I work for County Commissioner Sam John Boone and I am here with my friend who has a message for Harry the Cat Brecheen."

The nice lady was about my grandmother's age. She was dressed in a pink and white flowered dress and she had dark hair pinned up on the back of her head.

"He doesn't live here anymore," she said.

"What's the message?" I said fast to Mr. Mooney.

"Tell him Gertrude Williams Mooney is sorry about the hat."

The nice lady didn't get it. Neither did I.

"What hat?" I asked before she did.

"Gertrude and a friend took his hat. It was on a dare. Somebody dared them to swipe the hat off The Cat and they swiped it."

"When?"

"In St. Louis."

"How?"

"Years ago."

I looked at the nice lady with a silent plea to please, please understand what's going on here. Please, please just say the right thing, ma'am. The man's nuts but he's good.

225

"Well, I will certainly deliver the message," she said.

She went right up there on my hero list with Governor Allan Shivers of Texas.

There was a Thunderbird to Tulsa in ten minutes after we got back to the bus station. Mr. Mooney would change there to an American Bus Lines Inc. bus to Joplin. Mr. Starch was behind the ticket counter and made out the ticket.

"You were impressive with Roy and them at the Orpheum," he said to me, like it hurt to say it.

"Thank you, sir."

At the door to the bus, Mr. Mooney handed me a map. It was of Arkansas. As usual, a corner was torn off. It was the top right part from Jonesboro up to Paragould.

"How's your friend Pepper?" Mr. Mooney said.

"He's gone to heaven."

"Tell him to keep a look out for Gertrude. She'll be the pretty one with bangs in a white linen dress."

"I'll tell him."

Then he was gone.

I started to walk out to the street from under the covered driveway where the buses came. But it was too late to go anywhere right then.

God had decided on hail and rain for Adabel, Oklahoma, that afternoon.

I stepped back into the depot to have a seat until the storm passed.

A young two-eyed man was behind the ticket counter now with Mr. Starch. I watched them as Starch slowly went about showing the guy how to answer the phone, sell tickets, check baggage and do all the other things that I could already do better than anybody in the world.

It made Starch nervous for me to watch. I loved that. He

226

could have had me working behind that counter. Me, whose name was sung by Roy Rogers on the stage of the Orpheum Theater.

Me, whose only buddy was dead.

The next day I received my last letter from Pepper. It was on thin blue and red paper that was both the letter and the envelope.

Dear Mack:

I have never been so cold in my life. We're walking down a road from a place called the Chosin Reservoir. We just got up there two days ago. Now we're leaving. The Chinks are right on us. Guys are freezing their fingers and toes and heads off. Snipers pop us. Every once in awhile some mortar rounds come in. Our food is usually always cold. So is everything else.

Can't write much more now. My fingers are ice. So's my tail. You better spread the word there in Adabel to start learning Chink. Because if winning this war is up to me and the rest of us on this road then forget it. We're going to lose. That much is for sure.

Don't tell Jackie anything.

Your only buddy,
Pepper

The letter had a date on it that was two days before he died.

Pepper's body was brought to Adabel in a civilian black Cadillac hearse from Tulsa, where it had come on an airplane from San Francisco, where it had come on an airplane from

227

Korea. A Marine sat up front in the hearse with the driver. Two sailors and another Marine came with Sergeant Moyola in an Official Use Only Marine Ford Fairlane right behind.

They took the shiny brown metal casket to the same funeral home where Pepper said he threw up on the chest of a naked man. I still did not know if that really happened.

Brother Walt got the Marines to agree to let him instead of Jackie identify the remains. A next of kin was supposed to do it, but Brother Walt made them see that God would not want a pregnant wife to see the blown-up body of her dead husband.

The blown-up body of her dead husband.

Did they just throw the various parts of his body in the casket and close the lid? Or did they carefully reassemble him and lay him out in there with his head up at the top, then his neck and chest and arms going out and the stomach and then the legs and toes? Were there any parts they couldn't find? Were they sure the parts they found were really Pepper's?

What exactly does a hand grenade do when it blows you to bits?

Brother Walt put on a very nice funeral service for Pepper. It was in the big First Church of the Holy Road sanctuary. Only a dozen or so people were there, mostly folks from the rooming house and the coffee shop. The sailors and the Marine helped Sergeant Moyola and some American Legion men carry the casket in and out of the church and then blow a bugle and fire off some shots at Oak Lawn Cemetery.

Oak Lawn was just south of downtown. The Marine Corps paid for the cemetery plot and for the funeral, two wreaths of pink, red, yellow and white flowers and everything else that cost money.

Brother Walt, the Second Son of God, prayed for Pepper's soul and for Jackie's loss. He asked that she and all the rest of us who loved Pepper, which meant only me, be delivered the strength to understand why Pepper had been taken from us and to explain it someday to his child.

Here's the way it was, little Pepper Junior. Your daddy was a Bad Bowen. He was arrested on warrants from fourteen counties in three states. The only way he could keep from going to jail in most of those places was to join the U.S. Marines. The government figured anybody who was willing to be a Marine couldn't be all bad and deserved a break. But there happened to be a war on. It was in Korea, a place far away that nobody had ever heard of except the Koreans, the Chinese Communists and President Truman. Your dad went there and jumped on a hand grenade. It exploded and blew him to bits. Those bits are now buried at Oak Lawn Cemetery in Adabel, Oklahoma.

Any questions, little Pepper Junior?

16
Fizz

Love was something I knew absolutely nothing about. All I had really done was see my dad and mom love each other. He looked at her like he wanted to gobble her up, like she was something special to eat like a double hot fudge sundae. He always, always grinned when she came into a room. He tickled her by blowing in her ear, he made her laugh by doing an imitation of Jack Benny. He'd yell, "Rochester!" every time she'd ask him to take out the trash, for instance. He didn't sound a bit like Jack Benny, which she always told him, and which was the real reason it was so funny and why she laughed.

It never made any sense to me other than that they were in love.

I knew she loved him back because of the way she touched him. Her fingers glided over a hand or arm or cheek of his or through his hair like they were wands delivering special magic in slow motion. She touched my sister Meg and me and everybody else the regular way.

Meg had her own reasons for knowing Mom and Dad loved each other. Meg hated doing the laundry more than anything, so Mom's washing and ironing Dad's uniform shirts was it. He had only three of those gray shirts and that meant Mom was doing up one of them at least every three days. They had to have military creases down the front and back, so it was no easy job.

The capper for me was that they spent a lot of time in the bathroom together. That would take much love.

I wanted to ask both of them how they knew they loved the other. What had falling in love been like? Exactly what happened? Was there a voice that said, Trooper, you are in love with this wonderful woman. Margaret Ann, this trooper is your life's love. Was it something you felt or something you decided? Did it happen the first time you saw him—or her? The second, the third, the fourth? Did you decide, I cannot live my life from this day forward unless I can live it with this person? Did you dream about it? Day dreams and night dreams? Were there . . . well, dirty thoughts connected with it?

Mom died before I got around to asking her. The right time never seemed to come up for me to ask Dad.

So that had left my love education pretty much to the movies, comic books and, mostly, to guys I knew. A jerk in junior college told me you'd know you were in love when you heard Jo Stafford singing in your ear every time you were around a particular girl. Another guy said it had to do with breathing. If you couldn't catch your breath around her, it was love. There were also theories about itches under the left arm, rashes in the crotch, thumps in the stomach and elsewhere, incredibly long and riverlike wet dreams, unexplained coughs, fits of profanity.

The dumbest thing was what Randy, my St. Louis Cardinals–fan friend at Carrie Nation, said. He claimed his Methodist Sunday school teacher told him there was an ultimate question to ask yourself. Could you imagine lying down naked next to her on the grass in the middle of Garrison Field, our football stadium, with 5,143 people in the stands watching and cheering? If you were willing to do that, it was love, he said. If not, keep looking. The idea was an incredibly stupid joke but I couldn't help from that day on looking at girls and asking myself that question.

I might have been willing to do it for and with Lana Turner or somebody like that, but not girls I had ever met in person except Jackie.

I knew I was in love with Jackie the second I laid eyes on her in that Leavenworth café. Pepper spoke up about his love first. But I know I beat him to it inside my heart and soul. There was something that just went off in me that said, This Is It. This Is The Girl. This Is The One. I would have been willing to lie down in the center of Garrison Field with her.

But for Jackie the fall had been for Pepper, not me. Now Pepper was dead and she turned to me.

We were walking down Tulsa Avenue. It was sixty-four days after Pepper's funeral. We had just seen my friends Roy and Dale in their latest movie at the Orpheum.

"I went to the doctor today, Mack," Jackie said just as we got to the Rexall. "He thinks I'm going to have twins."

"God is Great!"

"Twins. Two people are in here." She patted her stomach, which was beginning to pooch out. She was wearing a blue-and-green-checked summer maternity dress I had given her as a special present. Brother Walt's wife and some other ladies at the church had also given her a few maternity things to wear.

"That means two baseball gloves, two Louisville Sluggers, two Roy Rogers cap pistols, two of everything. Maybe one of them will be a southpaw."

"Maybe one or both of them will be girls, too," she said. "So don't be going out and buying all boy stuff."

We turned at the corner with Broadway for the final six-block walk to her apartment.

"I want my babies to have a daddy, Mack. I want them to have you as their daddy."

My feet stopped moving. So did my breathing.

She put her hands up to my cheeks like my head was a golden cup of jewels. "Will you marry me, dear Mack?"

I put my arms around her and hugged her to me for dear, dear life.

And before long I felt something kicking my stomach. It had to be one of those two kids. Probably the southpaw. It was the most wonderful thing that had ever happened to my stomach or any other part of me.

When I got back to my rooming house that night I went right to the bathroom. There was no line. I went to the mirror and pulled the eyepatch away from my left eye socket.

It was still empty.

Jackie didn't love me. But she wanted to marry me.

Pepper fell on a hand grenade in a war he didn't even know about and I got the woman I loved.

I hated myself for being so happy about it.

Brother Walt, the Second Son of God, told me later it was God's will. He said Pepper would have wanted it this way, too. I didn't really believe that, but it was nice to hear and it made me feel better.

I decided making guilty people feel better was part of what following the Holy Road to Glory was really all about anyhow.

I wrote a letter to Pepper's dad at Leavenworth. It was the first letter I had written to anybody besides Pepper since Dad made me write a thank-you note to Grandmother Russell the Christmas after Momma died.

Dear Mr. Bowen:

You may not remember me but I am the one-eyed guy with the eyepatch and the funny hat who came with your late son Pepper to visit you awhile back. I know the Marine Corps told you about what happened to Pepper. It's an awful thing and I want you to know it was as sad for me as it would have been if he was my brother. I loved him like a brother. I guess you also know he was a hero. A Marine is coming down here soon to present some medals to Jackie, his wife. They're going to give her a Navy Cross and a Purple Heart at a Armistice Day ceremony in front of the courthouse. The whole town of Adabel, Oklahoma, will be there. You should be very proud, Mr. Bowen.

There are also two pieces of news that I would like to tell you about. First, you are going to be a grandfather in January. Jackie is going to have a baby. Maybe even two because the doctor thinks there's a good chance of twins. Think about having two little Bell Peppers running around down here in the Sooner State of Oklahoma! Second, I have been asked by Jackie to take Pepper's place as her husband so her children will have a father around. I have said yes, and I said it with high pleasure and happiness. I have always loved her with all my heart and soul. I hope you don't mind. The last thing Pepper said to me was for me please to take care of Jackie if anything happened to him.

I never had the honor of meeting your wife, Pepper's mother, so I am not writing to her. I would appreciate it if you would tell her this news. Thank you.

I am so sorry for you that Pepper was taken from us before he could become the lieutenant governor of Oklahoma. He would have been great at it. Maybe something else will come your way.

Sincerely yours,
The One-Eyed Mack

Dad's supervising lieutenant with the Kansas State Highway Patrol was a guy named Siloam. Dad and the others called him Suggestion Sy because he was full of suggestions. I don't even know what his real first and second names were. He must have had some. His mom and dad could not have named him Sy Siloam. Although it was even harder to imagine him having a mom and dad. He was not the kind of guy I could see ever running home in the afternoon with his report cards or sitting in somebody's lap or allowing anybody to wipe his nose or tie his shoes. It wasn't that he was a monster or anything like that. He was just distant. Very distant. When he came over for dinner when he was in town on an inspection trip, I always had the feeling he was really in Fort Scott or Topeka or Lawrence or some other place than there at our dinner table eating our meatloaf and boiled potatoes. Dad would ask him how the traffic was on the new

Highway 66 four-lane going across the Missouri line at Galena and he would clear his throat and light a cigarette and say something like, "We should have two more portable spotlights at the Galena office" or, "Does it look like headquarters is going to approve two weeks' vacation for everyone after three years?" or, "I would suggest the Ozarks over Kansas City as a vacation spot no matter the amount of time." Once he asked me what position I played in baseball. Second base, I said. "Remember to always hit the bag first with the right foot on the double-play pivot," he said. He asked Meg if she liked arithmetic. Yes, she said. "I would suggest you learn how to divide by four in your head and on your feet because so many things are divided into fours."

I bring him up only because of what he said one night about inspiration. Dad had complimented him again for having another good idea that won the fifteen-dollar monthly Trooper Suggestion Box Award. He had won it five out of the last six months, twelve of the last fourteen, twenty-two of the last twenty-five. His latest winning suggestion came to him while he was talking to a speeder he had stopped on U.S. 54 between Eureka and Yates Center. It was raining a storm and he looked down and saw that his spit-shined black uniform shoes were getting wet, muddy and ruined. He had an inspiration then and there that all patrolmen be issued rubber boots to wear in bad weather. He told headquarters in Topeka it would save wet wear-and-tear on their shoes but it would also make troopers less likely to avoid going outside to do their duty when it was raining, hailing or snowing because it would ruin their shines.

"Inspiration is like fizz in a bottle of Coca-Cola," was how he explained his powers of suggestion. "You never know how much is there till you pop off the lid."

My inspiration lid popped off one morning on the front lawn of the courthouse. I was on the way to the pick-up spot where Commissioner Sam sent a truck every morning at 7:15 to pick up all of us without cars and take us to the road barn.

I smiled and said good day to the World War One statue as I had come to do every morning. But it was different. He wasn't alone anymore. Not quite. There next to him on the next pedestal thing was a tall thin wooden box. The World War Two statue had finally arrived from Raleigh. He was there under the wood.

I kept walking.

Pop went the inspiration lid.

There's going to have to be a statue for our Korean War dead next, isn't there?

Fizz.

Why not make it a statue of Tom Bell Pepper Bowen? Fizz!

I had never paid much attention to Armistice Day before. It meant only that we didn't have to go to school, every man who had been in the service talked about it like it was yesterday, and there was a parade of veterans through downtown with the Carrie Nation Hatchet band leading the way. The only person who tried to make it special was my tenth-grade history teacher, Miss Johnston from Hutchinson, the salt capital of the world and home of the Kansas State Fair. She gave us a talk once about how many brave Americans had died in wars but none of it ever sunk in very far. No member of my family or any neighbor's or close friend's had been killed in World War Two or any other war, so I saw it mostly as a Randolph Scott–Tyrone Power problem.

It had sunk in now. There I sat on a folding chair on a

wooden stage with Commissioner Sam, the Marine captain from Tulsa, Jackie, Brother Walt, some elderly veterans and several judges and local officials of Adabel, Oklahoma. To our left was my friend the World War One statue looking proud and ready for the day. Next to him stood the World War Two statue on his pedestal. The wooden box had been removed but he was still covered with a large blue sheet of cloth. Nobody except Commissioner Sam and a few other dignitaries had actually seen the statue. Its unveiling was to be one of the morning's ceremonies. Another was honoring Adabel's oldest living veteran, a man who had fought in the Spanish-American War. Another was giving Pepper's medals to Jackie.

Another was me making the first public speech of my life.

It was a beautiful Oklahoma day. The sky was solid blue. The temperature was just warm enough to bring a little sweat under the arms. There was a smell of flowers from the hundreds of red, violet, pink, blue, yellow and white ones in beds all around the courthouse. I didn't know enough about flowers to even know what kind they were.

Not everybody in Adabel was there, but almost. In all directions there were only people to see.

Commissioner Sam was the master of ceremonies, and the first thing he did was invite Brother Walt to give the invocation. There were loudspeakers all out through the trees and in the streets and I am sure people as far as Atoka forty miles away could hear that booming bellow of the Second Son of God.

"Dear Lord and Savior, hear us! We gather here on this day to let our hearts and our minds cry out, Why? Why, oh, why did it have to be our loved ones who died? Why, oh, why was it our Americans who died to protect America while others lived? This is not a celebration of war here this morning, dear Lord, this is a ceremony of sadness. Help us through it. Help us in this as you do in all else. Dear Lord and Savior, hear us because we pray to you in your name. . . . Amen."

He said it "Ahhh . . . Men," with a heavy and rising hit on "Men." Just the way his dad, God, taught him to. Personally.

The Spanish-American War vet was in a uniform that I guessed was what he wore then. There were medals on his chest. He was an old man who stooped when he walked but otherwise seemed healthy and with it. The head of the local American Legion made a flowery introduction, the old man stood up and waved his hat to the crowd and sat back down. That was it.

I wondered why there wasn't a statue here on the courthouse lawn of a Adabel boy who had died in his war. It didn't seem fair.

The unveiling of the World War Two statue was next. The American Legion man, Commissioner Sam and the mayor of Adabel, a man named Mark Marshall McMillan everybody called Three M, did it. Commissioner Sam, in his whisper, read from the dedication on the pedestal and then the other two pulled the blue cloth down and off the statue.

There were appreciative gasps, then applause, and the Adabel High School Coyotes Marching Band played "Anchors Aweigh."

He was a sailor in full uniform with his round hat down at an angle over his right eye. He had his left hand in the pocket of his pea jacket with the right hand cupped up and across his forehead like he was looking for enemy ships out across the courthouse lawn to the ocean. His eyes were opened wide and his face was serious, almost exactly like that on the World War One soldier.

Hi, sailor. See you every morning just after seven.

The Marine captain from Tulsa was the same Marine captain from Tulsa who had brought us the news of Pepper's death. Now he was bringing us Pepper's medals. He was tall and handsome and stood up straight like Marines are supposed to stand. I had barely noticed what he looked like the first time. His hair was palomino white like Trigger's and I guessed him to be about thirty-five years old. I wondered suddenly if he had a wife and twins. What was he doing in Tulsa anyhow? Why wasn't he over in Korea falling on hand grenades himself?

He was speaking into the microphone, reading an official citation from the President of the United States or somebody.

"... For conspicuous gallantry and intrepidity at the risk of his life above and beyond the call of duty while serving as a Browning Automatic Rifleman of Company B, First Battalion, Seventh Marines, First Marine Division in action against enemy aggressor forces in Korea. His squad was advancing against heavy enemy small arms and mortar fire when a hostile hand grenade landed in front of him. He yelled 'Grenade!' to the other men. They hit the ground. He fell on the deadly missile without regard to his own personal safety. He was mortally wounded. His action saved his comrades in arms from serious injury or possible death. Private Bowen's heroic actions served to inspire all who observed them and reflect the highest credit upon himself and the United States Marine Corps and the Naval Service.

"He gallantly gave his life for his country."

He paused. Then turned around to Jackie.

"Mrs. Bowen, if you will please come forward at this time."

Jackie stood and walked up to the podium. She was wearing the same black dress the women at the coffee shop had picked out for her to wear to the funeral. Those twins were beginning to show but she looked great. She was not crying.

The captain handed her the Congressional Medal of Honor in a small carrying case.

"With it, Mrs. Bowen, by order of the President of the United States, I also present to you the Purple Heart medal," the captain said into the microphone.

Jackie accepted the Purple Heart in a case, shook his hand and walked back to her seat.

The Marine captain sat down too, and Commissioner Sam introduced me as a proud member of his county road crew and a friend of Private Bowen who has some closing remarks.

A friend of Private Bowen who has some closing remarks.

Brother Walt had gotten Commissioner Sam to agree to put me on the program. He also helped me with what to say and how to say it. "Think of somebody who loves you and get up there in front of all those people and give that speech like it's only to that one person who loves you," he said. "It would also help to try and imagine that person is in Atoka, so speak up."

My lip began twitching before Commissioner Sam finished his introduction. It was only six or seven steps from my chair to the microphone and podium but on the way my left leg started shaking. I arrived and felt like my whole body was lurching around like a drunk out of control, with my ears bouncing around off the top of my head, my hair falling out and in, my arms fighting to get out of their sockets, my good right eye getting ready to roll out on the lectern.

Then I realized what was going on elsewhere. The people

of Adabel were cheering and applauding me. Wildly. Like I was the hero. Like I was a star.

Yes, like I was the guy who appeared on the Orpheum stage with Roy, Dale, Gabby and Trigger.

The twitching and the shaking and the lurching and the shuddering stopped.

"My fellow Adabelites," I said all the way to Atoka. "I am here to say for Mrs. Bowen and for the memory of her husband how much we appreciate this special morning. Nothing will ever erase the sadness in our hearts for his loss but this morning will help us begin to understand what he died to protect...."

The people cheered me like what I had just said was the most brilliant thing they had ever heard. Even with the noise I thought I could still pick up a trace of my voice bouncing in and around the trees and the parked cars and the buildings and maybe all the way to Atoka. It was the voice of Randolph Scott. Solid, quiet, U.S. marshal, important.

"... It is fitting and appropriate that we all begin to think of erecting a third statue here on this hallowed ground to honor the Adabel dead in the Korean War. It is a great pleasure and honor for me to hereby propose that the statue be a likeness of the young hero we honor this morning— Tom Bell Bowen, Private, United States Marine Corps."

There was clapping and whistling and hooting and I felt like I was the Third Son of God.

After a minute or two I closed it off by saying:

"Thank you very much. And while we're at it, why don't we put one up for the Spanish-American War, too?"

I turned away, went over and shook the hand of the old Spanish-American War veteran and returned to my seat as the crowd roared on and on.

* * *

I had never in my life seen a human being as angry as Commissioner Sam was at Brother Walt and me. He had said just after he closed off the ceremony that he wanted to see us both right now in the sheriff's office inside the courthouse and he would not take no for an answer.

"You'll not get away with this," was the first thing he said right to Brother Walt once we closed the door.

"Now, Sam, what's . . ."

"Your Tom Bell Bowen was a wanted outlaw in fourteen counties in three states. He had more warrants out for his arrest than Billy the Kid and John Dillinger put together. Both his momma and his daddy are now residents in federal penal institutions. There is no way we are going to put his statue on the lawn of the courthouse in Adabel, Oklahoma. He's not even really from here."

"The boy died a hero, Sam. You heard the citation that Marine officer just read."

"No way, Walt. No way."

"God is Great."

"God isn't going to get His way this time. I don't care if you tell every Holy Road in the county to vote against me, I am not budging. As long as I am a county commissioner that is the way it is going to be."

"Maybe we'll just have to let the people decide this one," said Brother Walt with a huge grin. I may have been hearing things but I swear I heard a pop and a fizz. "It was the democratic form of government that Tom Bell Bowen died to preserve."

"I don't follow you," said Commissioner Sam. "The people are not going to vote on who's going to be the Korean War statue. . . ."

"But they're going to vote on their county commissioner. The young One-Eyed Mack here has just decided to run against you in the next election. Right, Mack?"

"Yes, sir," I said.

"God is Great," said Brother Walt.

"You're fired!" Commissioner Sam yelled at me in his loudest whisper.

"God is Great," I said.

Epilogue: Whatever Happened to the Trooper's Kid Who Called Himself The One-Eyed Mack?

Nothing bad has happened to me since.

The very next morning Mr. Starch, whose real name was Mr. Henderson, called me at the boardinghouse and said that ticket agent's job had come vacant again. The people of Thunderbird Motor Coaches would love to have a friend of Roy Rogers behind their ticket counter in Adabel, Oklahoma, he said. I was there making out a OW-2 ticket to Fayetteville, Arkansas (Thunderbird to Texarkana, Crown Coach to Fayetteville), within three minutes after we both hung up.

Then the next day Brother Walt came by during my thirty-minute lunch break and took me over to the courthouse to file as a candidate for county commissioner in the Democratic primary. There weren't any Republican voters or candidates in Adabel so the primary was all there was. The Adabel *Post-Times* kept calling it "tantamount to election," which must have meant the same thing to people who knew what *tantamount* meant.

The bus station was heaven, just like I always knew it

would be. It was big-time to pick up the ringing telephone and say, "Thunderbird Motor Coaches . . . May I help you?" and never know what the caller would want to know some bus thing about. When does the next bus go to Camden, Maine? What's the round-trip fare to Opelousas, Louisiana? Can I just ship a suitcase of clean laundry to my son at O-State in Stillwater without going on the bus myself? How long does it take to go to Bozeman, Montana? Does the bus go direct to Tucumcari, New Mexico, or do you still have to change in Ardmore, Dallas and Amarillo? My husband's sister left Duluth, Minnesota, Thursday morning at eleven, so what day and time will she get to Adabel? Does The Thunderbird run all the way to Pensacola, Florida? There was also big-time challenge and mystery to opening up those thick national tariff books and the up-to-date *Russell's Official National Motor Coach Guide* to figure out to the penny what the fare was and to the minute what the schedule was to any place in the United States of America. And my Randolph Scott voice was big-time perfect for droning smartly into the PA system microphone: "May I have your attention, please. . . . This is your first call for The Thunderbird to Oklahoma City . . . now leaving in lane one for Coalgate, Davis, Pauls Valley, Norman and Oklahoma City . . . connecting in Davis for Chickasha, Lawton, Waurika and Wichita Falls . . . connecting in Oklahoma City for Yukon, El Reno, Enid . . ." and the rest of the world.

Starch put me on the early shift so I would have my evenings free to campaign against Commissioner Sam John Boone. Starch said he was nonpartisan but accommodating me was the least he could do for democracy and Roy. He didn't think I had a chance of winning. Neither did I.

Campaigning meant mostly shaking hands and going to

church suppers and meetings at the fire house and in living rooms. I told everybody how important it was to remember our Spanish-American and Korean War dead with statues and I promised to erect them on the courthouse lawn with their help and God's blessing. I also promised to keep gravel on the gravel roads and blacktop on the blacktop ones. Most of the questions were about what it was like for me that night on the Orpheum stage with Roy, Dale, Gabby and Trigger.

Commissioner Sam put up scads of yard signs and posters about himself but he ignored me most of the time, except to tell the *Post-Times* a time or two that my idea for two more war-dead statues was fine with him. I thought he would come out and talk about Pepper's criminal background but Brother Walt kept telling me to relax, because not even Commissioner Sam was stupid enough to attack a dead Marine hero with a pregnant widow. "Politics sometimes makes people smarter than they are," said Brother Walt, the Second Son of God.

I won the election by fifty-eight votes. Commissioner Sam got 2,187 to my 2,245.

I was sorry to leave the ticket counter but the voters of Adabel had spoken and I answered their call. It made me the youngest person ever elected county commissioner in the history of the Sooner State of Oklahoma. Mr. Henderson Starch was very excited for me and said not to worry about leaving him just a few months after taking the job. He said there was a nasty rumor around that Continental Trailways was sniffing to buy out The Thunderbird anyhow.

I was also the first county commissioner in Sooner State history who didn't have a left eye. But I got that eye back two years later. Kind of. And it didn't have a thing to do with Jackie's love.

The guy we hired to make the statue of Pepper was the

same sculptor in Raleigh, North Carolina, who had made the one of the World War Two sailor. He came to Adabel and spent almost three weeks talking to Jackie and me about what Pepper looked like. None of us ever had a camera so there were no photographs. So that meant we had to describe him to the sculptor over and over in a lot of detail. He drew sketches and we looked at them and said, no, not quite like that, he'd draw some more and so it went. Finally he left for Raleigh to sculpt.

Brother Walt and I were the first to look at the finished statue. We took the wooden box off and saw a fabulous life-sized replica of a U.S. Marine in Korean War battle dress— helmet, boots, pack, cartridge belt, the whole thing. He was holding a Browning Automatic Rifle in both hands across his chest just as I had requested. It was perfect except for one problem. The face wasn't Pepper's.

It was mine.

The sculptor obviously couldn't figure out what Pepper looked like so the idiot put my face on it. The only thing different was the eyes. He gave me two of them. I was upset that it was me instead of Pepper and I was ready to send it back to Raleigh immediately to have the face changed. "Relax, Commissioner Mack," said Brother Walt. "God makes people blind to what they do not want to see. Nobody will see in this face what we see."

That statue of Pepper with my face and two eyes stands now on our courthouse lawn along with the World Wars One and Two and the Spanish-American one the North Carolina guy did a year after Korea. I hated the fact that the old Spanish-American vet on the Armistice Day stage that day died six months before we got it up.

I can see the four statues from my office window at the

courthouse. I'm looking at them right now, in fact.

The twins are six years old and they are dynamite kids. Tommy Walt can already hit the high hard one and make the double-play pivot at second base. His twin sister, Nancy Walterene, is the queen of the first grade and is about as smart a girl as I have ever known. Brother Walt, their god-father, says Tommy will end up an all-star second sacker in the National League and Nancy will probably grow up to be Oklahoma's first female county commissioner. Jackie and I have two other kids together as man and wife. Both are girls and both are as cute as anything female I have ever seen. Stephanie is four and Cathy is almost two and a half. Jackie no longer works full-time at the coffee shop but she does fill in as hostess sometimes during emergencies. She spends most of her time seeing to the kids or to her volunteer work with the Adabel Women's Garden Club and to teaching the Young Adults Class at the First Church of the Holy Road. We live in a great house on Choctaw Avenue just north of downtown. It has four good-sized bedrooms, a den which we use mostly as a playroom, a dining room, two bathrooms and all the rest. The backyard is where I cook out on a charcoal grill Jackie gave me for Christmas two years ago. It's also where I taught Tommy how to hold a bat and make the throw to first.

Jackie has been saying for almost six and a half years now that she loves me. I believe her although nothing has happened to the left eye socket. It's still empty.

I really like being county commissioner. I've already been reelected once and it was by over 500 votes. It's hard to imagine anybody coming along and beating me but I'm sure that's what Commissioner Sam thought, too, before I did it to him. Politics is a lot like what Suggestion Sy Siloam said about inspiration. The only difference is that in politics it's usually somebody else who pops the lid to see how much fizz you've got.

It isn't in the league with being Stan the Man but I think I've done very well with myself. Harry the Cat Brecheen retired from baseball after the 1953 season. He returned to Oklahoma but not to Adabel. I've met him several times and we know each other.

God tried throwing us a curve last year on Brother Walt. He had him suffer a heart attack while performing the rite of full-immersion baptism on five ninth-graders. Brother Walt, now fifty-six years old, survived beautifully, of course, and is back at it at full God-is-Great speed. The whole thing was just God's way of trying to throw us off the track by making us think Brother Walt was mortal like the rest of us. It didn't work. I know he's the Second Son of God and I know he will live forever.

I must say, though, that Jackie and the kids and I don't see much of Brother Walt anymore. Once we started being predictably good Holy Road–type people he pretty much dropped us from his schedule and agenda. "Good people are no fun, no meatloaf for me," he said.

The Thunderbird has already ended up not living forever. Continental Trailways did buy them out. Most of the schedules they run in here now are through buses between Tulsa north and Dallas south. They've lost the personal touch The Thunderbird had.

Pepper's dad never answered my letter. We have not heard a word of any kind from his mother or any other kin either. I do keep expecting somebody to show up someday out of the blue and announce they are the mother, brother, cousin, uncle or something of Tom Bell Pepper Bowen. I don't know what they'll want or say, but not knowing things like that is the real fizz in the Coca-Cola bottle.

My dad is now the sergeant in charge of the Kansas State Highway Patrol district in Emporia. Meg stayed in town and is the assistant cashier at the Farmers and Drovers. They're both very proud of me being a county commissioner, no question about it. We all get together four or five times a year either here in Adabel or in Kansas. Meg is married to the butane-gas dealer but they do not yet have any children. They will soon, though, I am sure. Meg sure does love ours and so does her husband, Paul.

One last thing.

There was a story in last Sunday's *Daily Oklahoman* in Oklahoma City about the next elections. It said several important party officials in Oklahoma City and Tulsa are looking for a "fresh face" to run for lieutenant governor on the main slate.

They quoted some anonymous person saying there was a young county commissioner down in Adabel they might check out because he had made quite a name for himself building statues of the war dead.

Lieutenant governor of Oklahoma?